Rebirth

S.E. Wendel

EARTH ALIENS

EPIC
Press

Rebirth
Earth Aliens: Book #6

Written by S.E. Wendel

Copyright © 2016 by Abdo Consulting Group, Inc.

Published by EPIC Press™
PO Box 398166
Minneapolis, MN 55439

All rights reserved.

Printed in the United States of America.

Cover design by Dorothy Toth
Images for cover art obtained from iStockPhoto.com
Edited by Clete Barrett Smith

LIBRARY OF CONGRESS CATALOGING-IN-PUBLICATION DATA

Wendel, S.E.
Rebirth / S.E. Wendel.
p. cm. — (Earth aliens ; #6)
Summary: The human domination of Terra Nova is nearly complete, the natives
routed, their queen taken prisoner, and the peace movement suppressed. But when
Zeneba returns to defend her people against extinction, she leads the charge in the
battle that will decide who will be rulers of Terra Nova.
ISBN 978-1-68076-027-9 (hardcover)
1. Aliens—Fiction. 2. Human-alien encounters—Fiction.
3. Extraterrestrial beings—Fiction. 4. Science fiction.
5. Young adult fiction. I. Title.
[Fic]—dc23
2015903971

EPICPRESS.COM

To my father, who has graciously accepted that I will never be a pro-golfer

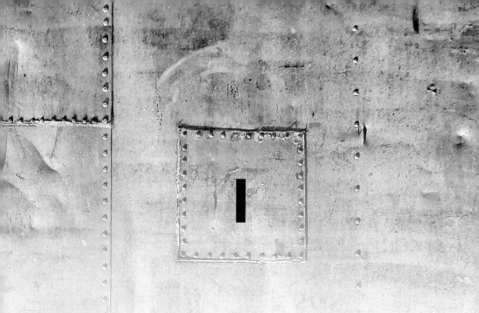

Rhys O'Callahan slammed his fist on the table. "That isn't good enough!"

The others of the resistance looked at him. They all seemed tired. The weeks since the Battle of San Angelo, as it was being called, had been hard on all those in New Haven, especially those who still stood against a triumphant General Hammond, the corrupt leader of their military dictatorship. Crackdowns had begun—if they thought things were bad before, it was nothing compared to now.

Rhys had noticed a thinned crowd when he arrived for the meeting. Even he had trouble navigating the streets of New Haven undetected; he was adept at hiding in shadows, making himself invisible, but still he doubled back at least twice to avoid patrols. Hammond's watchdogs were everywhere, but Rhys sauntered into the meeting nonetheless.

He had to say his peace.

Ulysses Carter, the leader of the resistance movement against General Hammond, gazed steadily at Rhys, his large, dark hands folded neatly in front of him. Rhys didn't like Carter gauging how much more of a petulant child he was going to be that night. Going on fourteen, Rhys was easily the youngest person in the room.

"I agree something has to be done," Carter said finally. "But I don't know that now's the time. We've only just been able to reestablish connections."

"You're scared," Rhys hissed. "You all are."

"Of course we are," said Jana, Carter's second.

"We've got the same reason to fear Hammond as the natives do. Her guns," said another; Rhys didn't catch who.

He ground his teeth. "Well that gives us a common enemy."

"Rhys, listen to me," Carter said with enough gravity to make Rhys's anger cool a moment. "What you're asking for is both noble and stupid. Granted, those usually go together, but right now, I just don't see how we can free her."

Not the answer Rhys wanted, he shoved a hand in his hair and began to pace. He had been there, at the battle, had marched on San Angelo with the Charneki army. Upon arriving on Terra Nova, their new planet, humans had soon realized they weren't alone—two native species already inhabited the planet, the Charneki and the Tikshi, though the Tikshi lived on a separate jungle subcontinent. Rhys had spent the past winter as the Charneki queen's prisoner and guest.

It had been Rhys's hope to avoid this war. Almost two years ago he befriended the queen's younger brother, Zaynab, before the young Charneki was slain. This bond made him believe peace could exist between Charneki and humans, and so when a delegation was put together to broker such a peace, Rhys was anxious to go. Things hadn't gone according to plan, and it was only through hard work and a leap of faith on the queen's part that the humans hadn't been killed. In fact, if Rhys were back in their capital city now, he would be helping the others build generators for the Charneki.

His palms splayed on the table, Rhys leaned forward, trying to make himself look menacing, though he knew that was hard for his young face among adults.

"We've got to do something. Who knows what Hammond's doing to her?"

"She's definitely still alive," Jana said.

Rhys's nostrils flared. "Yeah, I'm sure she's living in luxury."

The Charneki queen had tried to attack San Angelo, the newer of the two human colonies, thinking it the weaker target. For a while it looked like the Charneki might succeed with their sheer numbers, but when General Hammond arrived with reinforcements, the native army was routed and the queen captured. She sat now in New Haven's prison.

"Even if we could get her out—and I'm not saying we can—what then? Return her? How do we know the natives will join us?" Carter asked.

"Of course we return her. She's a being, not a bartering chip."

Carter opened his mouth, but he never got his next sentence out.

The front door slid open, and before it was barely wide enough for a person to enter, Cassandra Tran burst into the room.

"The fox is coming for the hen house!" And then she was gone.

The room was eerily quiet for a long moment before erupting with activity, everyone headed en masse to the door. Feet pounded the stairs, bodies slipping quickly in the inky shadows of buildings and alleyways. Rhys avoided the lampposts, shrinking against the apartment building until he could feel his way around to a narrow lane leading away from that section of the residential quadrant.

His pulse thrummed in his ears as he made a break across open ground, heading for another apartment complex. The streets were deserted, the curfew strict.

He had almost made it across the empty courtyard, almost felt home free, when a pair of meaty hands whirled him around. He stared up into the face of Colonel Klein, General Hammond's second-in-command.

There wasn't time to say anything or even scream out before Klein began dragging him by his shirtfront towards the city square. Rhys fought him every step of the way, his eyes darting about, looking for any escape.

He could hear his brother's words in his head: "Keep a low profile, all right? Your age won't work for you forever." But Rhys couldn't stay quiet about this, not when he lay awake at night replaying the battle over and over again in his head. The queen had trusted him, had shown him and the others mercy. She protected him, maybe even cared for him. He had to get her out of there.

By the time he and Klein arrived at the square, others of the resistance had already been set on their knees, surrounded by soldiers. Other civilians, woken from their beds, stood at the outskirts of the square, looking on.

Rhys was pushed unceremoniously onto his knees beside Jana. They exchanged looks. He managed to see the others who had been caught and felt relieved it wasn't Carter or Cass—Carter because he was the brains of the operation and Cass because he liked her. Cass was a friend of his brother, Hugh, and had taken the reins of the science department from her former mentor, Dr. Oswald, who had been put to death for being a spy by the Charneki queen.

His breath came in ragged spurts as he looked

about him. He held hope there might be a way out, and he kept his eyes open for one. He had to get out of there—live to fight another day.

Unsure exactly why they were being kept in the square rather than carted off to a prison cell, Rhys felt an oncoming of dread. The general wouldn't dare kill other humans . . . would she? Her main platform was that human life was precious, so precious it warranted the extermination of another species to secure living room on Terra Nova. Could she betray that?

Klein stepped into the center of the square, looking out at the growing crowd of civilians. Rhys had the fleeting hope that if anything too drastic happened, the civilians might help them— they outnumbered military personnel ten to one. But when he glimpsed their shadowed face, Rhys knew he and the others were on their own. Even if the general didn't have their support, she still had them cowed.

"I want you to listen up!" Klein projected. "This

resistance wants to see the human race fail. They want to make us vulnerable. I'm going to show you just how much this will be tolerated."

He gave a nod, and the first resistance member was hauled up and beaten, punches and kicks landing on all parts of him. When the soldiers finished, he was a whimpering heap.

When it was Jana's turn, she looked at Klein defiantly, for as long as she could manage it, before succumbing to the obvious pain. She slumped down, barely conscious, and suddenly Rhys sat there all alone.

He looked around a moment when he wasn't immediately seized. The crowd murmured to themselves. Even Klein stood in conference with one of his officers, and Rhys realized what was going on.

"We could say he's young-looking for his age," he heard Klein say.

"I'm thirteen," Rhys said as loud as he dared. "Can the general afford such bad press? What will

San Angelo think of her?" He put on his best smirk to lather up the taunt.

The way he saw it, one of two things could happen: Klein could back down because of Rhys's age and the civilians' recognition of it, leaving Rhys unharmed, or Klein could have him beaten like the rest, which might unsettle the crowd enough for them to do something. Both seemed advantageous in their own ways, but Rhys decided he had better steel himself for the second option.

As Klein personally picked him up by his collar, Rhys thought with a cringe that he might have overplayed his hand.

"Stop! No!"

His heart beating quickly, Rhys looked around for the familiar voice. To his left, his brother, Hugh, was pushing through the soldiers. A mirror of what he would look like in seven years, Hugh and Rhys had been twins on Earth, but while Hugh had stayed awake during the seven-year journey to Terra Nova, Rhys had been put to cryogenic sleep with the other civilians and woke up still aged eleven. It had been strange, to say the least, waking up to find that Hugh was an adult.

"I can handle this," Rhys said as Hugh came running up, breaking through the line of soldiers.

He didn't mean to be gruff with Hugh—what he was doing was what Carter would call "noble and stupid." Though Rhys considered him more a stranger than a brother, Hugh had come looking for him in the battle, even taken an arrow for him in the back. Rhys knew he owed his brother, which was why he scowled to see him there now. It was bad enough without Hugh getting in trouble too.

"Get outta here, O'Callahan," Klein growled.

"Please, sir, he's just a kid. He doesn't know what he's doing," Hugh said breathlessly.

"This *kid* is in the resistance."

"I'll do anything you ask, Colonel, but please, just let my brother go. He won't do anything—I'll make sure of it."

"That time has come and gone. You had your chance to make him see. Now it's my turn."

Klein wound his fist, readying to strike, and Rhys closed his eyes tight, clenched all the muscles he could.

He stumbled, barely catching his footing as Klein released him. His eyes shooting open, Rhys stood, stunned, to see Hugh between him and the colonel, Hugh having pushed him away.

Klein reared on Hugh and would have crashed down on him if the crowd hadn't grown noisy. They must have seen Hugh's actions as heroic, and Rhys dared to hope he might be walking to a prison cell on his own two feet.

Looking about him, Klein seemed to know he risked a fight he couldn't win with his dozen soldiers. He turned his face to the nearest one and nodded. "Take them."

Hands seized Rhys, and he was pushed forward, out of the square. He craned his neck, trying to find Hugh. He caught his brother's gaze for a moment before being led off to a cell with his name on it.

———————

The *mara*, beloved by all Charneki, daughter of the suns, Nahara and Undin, sat in a cold cell wondering how her life had come to this. Her prison was a foreign one, all metal and sterile and not made for her tall, lithe Charneki body.

Zeneba shifted a little, trying but failing to make herself more comfortable. She instantly regretted her action, wincing at the pain that throbbed from her side. Looking down, she groaned to see another bloodied bandage.

The humans had patched her up well enough— they had also wounded her with their snarling, burning weapons in the first place.

The battle had been going well for the Charneki; they stood at a disadvantage with their wood and iron weapons, but their numbers and courage had been great. When she closed her eyes, she could see the battlefield stretched out before her. Her eyes shot open.

Her last moments of consciousness during the battle were the worst memories. She had been surrounded by her Guard, defending her to the last, when they were bombarded by a break-off unit of humans in their great metal vehicles. Her Guard clashed with them, fighting to keep them from her, but in the end the humans dragged her into the back of a metal beast. Her Guard was decimated, and the last thing she remembered was Ondra, her love, lying on the ground, face down.

Her head slumped back against the wall. Her body and soul were tired. She wanted to sleep but feared what would happen should she. This prison had eyes everywhere; if only this, that she knew. It wasn't like the dungeons of Karak, her beautiful mountain-city. It was well lit, never darkening, as if they didn't want her to sleep either.

She touched a three-fingered hand to the side

of her face, felt the lessening swell underneath her square eye. The wounds she incurred at the battle were healing—the Charneki tended to be fast healers, when treated with their own medicine, but her side-wound was fussy because it was apathetic human doctors, not her own physicians, treating her. The wounds she had from interrogation were newer, dark.

She thought with malice about that small room they sometimes took her to, where she was made to sit down. Across a small metal table—Sunned Ones above, could they not use anything else!—sat a female human, rather short as far as humans went. From her smug look, she seemed to take particular pleasure in seeing Zeneba sitting there, a captive, stripped of everything, her army, her armor, her dignity. Zeneba could only assume this was the humans' evil *mara* Rhys had told her about.

They were interrogations of some kind, and Zeneba learned quickly to say little. She received rough treatment no matter what she did, so she gave little away. From the snatches of conversation she caught between the humans, when the translator voice box wasn't turned off quickly enough, she deduced there was division amongst the humans. This was keeping Zeneba alive, forcing the human *mara* to use her other ways.

It gave Zeneba small pleasure to be as unhelpful as possible. Always they were questioning her, trying to find how she could help them win the war. She suspected the division ran deep, for it was enough to deter them from killing her outright, despite her lack of cooperation.

The more time she spent in this place, the more she wanted to burn it to the ground. If she had the will to speak, only curses would flow from her lips.

When it wasn't too painful to think about, her thoughts wandered to Karak, to Yaro, Ondra, Elder Zhora, Ankha. Did they miss her? Did they know she was alive in this hell?

She frowned to hear noise. She had long since figured out that she was the only one being kept in the prison; when others entered, it was to fetch her. Swallowing hard, she steeled herself.

Moments slipped by. More noise. She tried to stifle the panic rising in the back of her throat. What more could they do to her?

Her eyes went wide to see soldiers bearing other battered-looking humans into the cells across from hers. She sat in the last cell in a long, narrow, sickeningly well-lit corridor, and from the look of it, they were filling the other cells with humans.

What was going on?

Slowly, trying to move her chest as little as possible, Zeneba inched forward on her hands and knees. She couldn't stand to her full height, so she didn't try to.

Her eyes grew wide when she saw all the cells now occupied by humans, and she looked them over with horrified interest. They indeed seemed beaten, their skin bruised, their eyes, if open, rimmed in purple circles.

Zeneba's attention was caught by the last human

being pushed into the cell next to the one across from her. Two larger humans struggled against the other, this one putting up a fight whereas the others had simply slumped onto the small cots. Her mouth dropped open when, as the clear door to the cell slid closed and the two others stepped back, she saw it was Rhys.

She cried out his name.

His head jerked towards her, and he made a surprised sound. She couldn't believe the relief she felt seeing him.

One of the larger humans slammed their hand against the door. From its tone, Zeneba inferred they were giving Rhys a warning.

Rhys scowled, watching them walk back down the corridor, out of the prison. Then he turned his gaze back to Zeneba and pressed himself against the clear door. He smiled.

"I am happy to see you, *mara*," he said, having learned the Charneki language from Zeneba's brother Zaynab.

"I'm relieved to see you, little one," she said. "I didn't know what happened to you at the battle."

He opened his mouth, then closed it again, as if he were changing his answer in the middle of his thought. "I was found and taken to the city," he said.

She nodded, leaning against the wall. She rested her head against the door. "How many days has it been since the battle, Rhys? I've lost count."

"Two-and-twenty."

She closed her eyes. So long.

Both of them looked towards the mouth of the prison where more voices were heard. Zeneba noted the conflicted look clouding Rhys's face and wondered what he was thinking.

Another surprise was in store for her when a larger human stepped in front of Rhys's cell. This one wasn't in soldier's garb and carried themselves quite differently. When she caught a glimpse of its face, her curiosity piqued. It was like looking at an older Rhys.

The bigger human squatted down, balancing on the balls of the feet. It spoke soft words to Rhys, and Rhys looked pointedly down at the ground.

Zeneba couldn't tear her gaze from this new-comer. So like Rhys in looks, so different in manner. Could . . . could they brothers? She looked back and forth at them. They were the image of one another, and she concluded they had to be brothers. But Rhys had said he didn't have a family?

They looked like brothers, but their behavior wasn't evidence for it. Rather than looking at the other, they both stared at the ground, the other's chest, something over the other's shoulder. Her intense curiosity made her wish she spoke some of the human language—she could tell words for assent or decline, had learned the words for "sky," "stone," and others, but nothing that helped her make sense of their quiet conversation.

Whenever Rhys spoke it was through tight lips. His brother looked tired, as if he too hadn't slept in days. His face was shadowed in small, stubbly hair.

The brother placed his hand against the clear door.

Rhys looked at it a moment, his eyes glassy. He put his hand against the door too.

The brother nodded and stood. He said a few more quiet words.

Zeneba met his gaze when his eyes wandered to her. She got to look him full in the face and decided yes, they had to be brothers.

Something odd, like guilt, flashed across the brother's face and then he was gone from the prison.

She looked back at Rhys to find him deep in thought.

"What does this mean?" she asked him.

Rhys glanced at her before leaning his head back and closing his eyes. "It means she has won."

———

Plowing a hand through his hair, Hugh O'Callahan

tried to swallow his rising panic. He had put on a brave face for his brother, but now, as he left the prison, his head began swimming with worry.

He didn't get far before Colonel Klein stepped in front of him, and Hugh prepared himself.

"Your little stunt worked this time, O'Callahan, but the general won't stand for it for long, no matter what the civilians think."

"He's just a kid." Hugh's voice was hoarse, his throat barely working.

"That kid's causing a lot of problems." He leaned forward. "And so are you. If you put as much as a toe outta line, it'll be the end of the line for you two. I don't want to see anything like tonight ever again. If I do, your brother's the first person I visit. Do I make myself clear?"

"Yes, sir."

Colonel Klein looked him up and down before stepping out of Hugh's way. Klein's parting look told him to head straight home without further incident, and that's exactly what Hugh did.

His dark, empty apartment greeted him. Rhys's things lay strewn about his room, the door still open from when he left that evening. It had been a mixed bag of emotions, having Rhys home. While he sorely missed his brother, things between them were just as difficult as they had been before Rhys's capture. Maybe even worse.

Rhys watched what he said around Hugh, evidently unsure where Hugh's loyalty lay. It hurt Hugh to know Rhys didn't trust him. Hugh's loyalty was to his brother. And that was why he had to do as Klein said.

Sitting down at the table, Hugh rested his head in his hands, wrapping his fingers around clumps of hair. He sat there, staring at the tabletop, thinking, until gray dawn seeped through the windows.

He ran what happened in his head over and over again: the sickness he felt seeing Rhys about to be beaten, the pain at witnessing him get dragged to prison, the frustration at the wall between them even after all he had done.

As if sensing his thoughts, the wound he sustained from an arrow to the shoulder began prickling. He hadn't thought, just put himself between Rhys and a stray volley. He still couldn't believe he had walked right into the Battle of San Angelo, but the desire to help his brother was overwhelming. And he had paid the price for it.

Though this thought crept slowly into his head, his reaction was instantaneous. Jumping up from the table, Hugh checked the time on his gauntlet and left the apartment, hesitating only long enough to grab a flavorless protein pack from the sparse pantry.

Making for the northwest corner of the residential quadrant, Hugh struggled to keep his stride normal as he gnawed on his flavorless breakfast. The route was familiar to him by now; he took it almost daily to see his dying mentor. He almost stumbled at the word. Dying.

Mikhail Saranov had been Hugh's mentor during the seven-year journey to Terra Nova, had taught him everything about engines and engineering, had been a father to him. When asked, Saranov followed Hugh into the fray. He had gotten two arrows in the chest as thanks.

Walking into the medical ward, Hugh nodded at the familiar faces of the nursing staff. He passed by the doctor assigned to Saranov and regretted meeting her gaze.

"How's he doing today?" Hugh asked.

The doctor cleared her throat. "He's been asking for you."

She left him with that, and Hugh stood in the middle of the corridor, opening and closing his fists.

Slowly, he entered, finding Saranov in a soft slumber. He sat down next to him quietly, hating to wake him.

Though his wounds had been tended to quickly after the battle, Saranov needed immediate surgery, which he almost didn't survive. He lost a good deal of blood on the battlefield, even more on the operating table. Hugh would have cut open his arm right there if it would have helped him. The transfer back to New Haven's sick ward hadn't been easy on him, and a second surgery had gone almost as disastrously as the first. By now the doctors weren't sure anything could be done; his body was too weak.

Hugh touched a hand gently to Saranov's shoulder. "Hey there."

His intense blue eyes fluttered open, and Saranov blinked a few times before his vision focused. A slow grin spread over his face.

"Where've you been?" he said, barely more than a hoarse whisper.

"I'm sorry, I . . . it's Rhys."

Saranov frowned. "What now?"

"H-he's been thrown in prison, and I—" Hugh put his hand over his mouth to hold in his sob. Everything seemed to be crashing down around him—a brother in prison, a father dying in front of him.

Saranov put a hand on Hugh's head. "He's doing what he thinks is right. So should you."

"But what's that? I don't know anymore!" He leaned in closer, wanting, needing to tell his mentor everything but knowing there were eyes and ears everywhere. "I can't risk anything—I can't put him danger. They said I have to be loyal or else they'll—"

Saranov tightened his grip on Hugh's hair. "Listen to me now," he said, blinking a few times to regain focus. "I've spent too long worrying what *she'll* do."

Hugh stared at him. "What d'you mean?"

Saranov sighed and motioned for Hugh to move closer. When he had, he said, "Hammond will be the death of this colony. I've known it for years. And she knows I know."

"But then why—?"

"Because she threatened *you*. I wanted to mutiny against her when we were on the *Argo*, but she said if I tried anything, you'd pay the price. I couldn't let that happen. So I forgot what I thought. I did what she said to do, for you."

Hugh sat there, speechless.

A tear slipped out of Saranov's left eye. "I can't let you do the same thing. I can't let you live in fear."

Hugh shook his head. "But I can't let her hurt Rhys."

Saranov closed his eyes. "I couldn't let her hurt you. I don't regret what I did. I just can't stand to see her do this to you too. Hugh, I wasn't strong enough to take the risk. You need to be now. It might be the only way to save Rhys."

"I can't—I can't risk him!"

Saranov took a labored breath, and Hugh's own caught in his throat. Gripping the hand he offered, Hugh crushed Saranov's in his.

"I told you before that the time wasn't right—that you needed to bide your time to help your brother." His grip tightened. "Now's your time.

Take your life in your own hands. Make this a real New Earth. Do it for me."

"H-hey, c'mon now, you're gonna be here."

Leaning back, Saranov grinned as his eyes closed. "It's your life, Hugh."

Hugh watched the ball of Saranov's throat rise and fall as he swallowed, then he stilled. His hand fell slack in Hugh's.

Hugh opened his mouth to call for the doctor, but nothing came out. It wouldn't do any good. Not now.

Tears stung his eyes, blurring his vision though he couldn't look away from that face, tanned, lined. It had the potential to be stern but also gentle. Wrapping both hands around Saranov's, Hugh's forehead slumped against them.

He cried for him, for the years he should have lived if Hugh hadn't gone marching off into battle, for all the times he had been patient and kind to him. He cried because he knew, deep down, that he wasn't brave enough.

2

They came for her in the middle of the night—or what felt as such to Zeneba, for she had finally allowed her heavy eyes to ease shut. It seemed crueler to do this than to interrogate her. If only she could sleep. She caught small moments here and there, assured somehow by having Rhys near.

Two human soldiers stood at her door, and she didn't need the eerily toneless translation of their words to know she was to stand. She did so slowly, glaring at them as she stooped her head so that it wouldn't hit the ceiling.

The clear door slid open, and she stepped out

to find another broad human standing just a few paces away. Her upper lip twitched. Her interrogator. The male was tall for a human, with shoulders almost double the width of Zeneba's, yet she relished towering over him.

He jerked his head, leading her and the two soldiers out of the prison.

Her heart quickened when she heard noise behind her, and she looked over her shoulder to see the soldiers dragging Rhys out of his cell.

"Leave him be!" she cried, but hands seized her, pulled her out of the corridor.

Her interrogator seemed to take pleasure in striking her wounded midsection, and when she doubled over in pain, cloth came over her head to blind her. They roughly led her the fifty-seven strides to that dark, cavernous room where her interrogator seemed most at home.

Hands pulled her down, and she landed on a metal chair. She tried to move as little as possible, knowing there wasn't anything to see beyond the cloth. Sitting silently, she listened to the sound of bodies filling the room.

When the cloth finally came off her head, Zeneba was slow to open her eyes, letting them adjust to the one, disconcerting central light. She blinked. Frowned.

Sitting across the table was Rhys.

Her jaw set, and she slowly eased back in the chair, watching the others move about the room. More soldiers. Her interrogator. She focused on the human's *mara*.

As if to unsettle them further, her interrogator leaned forward with deliberate slowness to place a thin device on the table between her and Rhys. She knew from her previous times that it was the voice box.

The moment she believed it to be ready, she asked, "Why is the boy here? He's done nothing."

Her interrogator turned to face her, folding his hands behind his back. "He will speak for you to us," came the lifeless reply.

Zeneba frowned, nodding at the device. "You already can speak to me. Why is he here?"

She tried not to the let the human *mara* intimidate her as she leaned forward, her five-fingered hands splayed on the table. Zeneba met her gaze, her chin tilting upwards ever so slightly. There was no reason to be intimidated. She was Zeneba Mara the Golden-Hearted. This *mara* was nothing more than a human with a weapon.

"Do your people know you are alive? Will they fight for you?" the human *mara* finally said.

"My people are proud. They will fight for their homes."

She was ready for her interrogator's strike across her face, bit down on her tongue to keep from retaliating. The first time it happened, she struck back. That only got her a crescent bruise around her right eye. If she was to survive, and what was more, to keep them away from Rhys, she had to be smart.

"That is not what we asked."

Zeneba righted her face, gazing steadily at the human leader. "My people are proud. They will fight—"

A blow to her side this time, and she couldn't help crying out, the pain radiating out from the fussy wound. She clenched her teeth, steeled herself, knew she had to keep her wits.

The human *mara* slammed her hands on the table, but Zeneba was unimpressed. "Will they fight for you?" she demanded.

With sickening pleasure Zeneba lifted her head, her flaring nostrils the only indication of her wrath. That was the only answer this *plarra* would get from her. She knew they meant to use her—either force a surrender for her return or kill her in front of her people to send a message. She wouldn't help them decide which would be better, not when they seemed wracked with internal discord.

This time it was the human *mara* who lashed at her, hit her face, her shoulders, her chest, until Zeneba felt she would be purpled head to toe. Her swirls of iridescent skin rippled uninhibited into a fiery red, her will slipping. She had been trained for years by her Elders to control the *harn-da*, but she was losing her resolve. Nothing would please her more than to give in to her rage and beat this human.

Zeneba's head slammed down on the table, her pulse hammering when the device translated, "Give me your knife."

Rhys's chair went flying backwards as he jumped up, crying out, and it took two soldiers to get him back down again. As he struggled, tears pouring from his eyes, a flurry of human words came tumbling from his mouth, and Zeneba realized too late that it wasn't her being interrogated this time.

"They will do anything for her," the device said without Rhys's emotion. "She is everything to them. The Charneki will do anything you ask of them. I will do anything. Do not harm her."

She let out a painful breath as she rested her

head back on the table. It was cool, felt good against her hot, abused skin.

Rhys leaned forward towards her. "I am sorry," he said in Charneki. "Please, *mara*, forgive me."

She shook her head once, for that was all she could manage. What he spoke was true.

The human *mara* clapped her hands together. "Get me *Kimura*. Even he cannot argue with using her if it ends the war."

———

After rapping her knuckles against the door, Elena Ames shoved her hands in her jacket pockets and waited. Even though spring was thankfully here, New Haven was so far north that, while the terrain was finally turning green, it still felt chilly most of the time.

When the door to Hugh's apartment finally opened, she didn't wait for his greeting before pushing her way in, saying, "I've got a bone to pick with you."

"That can't be good," he said, closing the door. He sounded lackluster.

Turning around in his kitchen, she leaned against the countertop. "You have to know what's going on," she said, crossing her arms.

He nodded.

"Well what're we gonna do?"

"What d'you mean?"

She gawked at him. "Aren't you at all concerned that your brother's *in prison?*"

His gaze fell to the floor. "He survived native prison pretty well. Rhys will make it through."

Elena couldn't believe what she heard, and she couldn't make out whether that was because Hugh's words were the opposite of what she had expected, or that Hugh didn't believe it himself. His voice hadn't been very convincing—there was barely any trace of emotion in it, making her suspicious.

"Come again?"

He took a deep breath, still not looking at her. "He's done something wrong. He has to learn there're consequences to his actions."

"D'you hear yourself?" she demanded, poking his forehead roughly. "I can't believe you!"

She had had every intention of making plans with him about springing not only Rhys but the native queen as well. Though slow to come around, Elena had joined the opposition recently with the help of her and Hugh's friend, Cass. It went against her soldiering background, but she couldn't deny her feelings anymore. What General Hammond was doing was wrong.

She wasn't ready for Hugh's head shooting up with an expression between glaring and tears. "Can you leave it alone?" he asked, barely more than a whisper.

Elena's mouth hung open, and nothing came out.

He searched her face, but Elena didn't know for

what. His eyes became teary, and his head slumped down onto her shoulder.

She stiffened from the contact, never one for touching. His outpouring of emotion overwhelmed her. Not knowing what else to do with her hands, she put them lightly on his back.

"What's going on?" she murmured.

"S-Saranov died yesterday."

Elena's heart panged painfully, and her arms tightened around him. She couldn't imagine dealing with what he now had to—her own mentor during the expedition, Sgt. Rhiannon White, was the closest thing Elena ever had to a parent, and the idea of losing her made Elena queasy.

"I'm so sorry," she said. "Are you gonna be all right?"

He shook his head against her shoulder.

"What can I do?"

He sucked in a ragged breath. "Don't push me. I-I can't . . . "

She eased him back so that she could look at

him. "But he's your brother. You've gone through so much to get him back, and now you're just going to give up?"

"There's nothing I can do."

"That's not true."

He wiped at his face, frowning. "What d'you want me to do? Go to the opposition? They're the ones who got him into this mess."

She swallowed hard. She had come uncertain where exactly Hugh stood politically—she knew he didn't support Hammond's regime, but how active he was willing to be against her was up in the air. She thought he would do anything to help Rhys, and this sudden shift made her leery. Had they threatened him? Threatened Rhys? Even so, it still made her mad to see him bend.

That anger grew without her realizing it, and she said, more harshly than she meant to, "Rhys wouldn't just sit around doing nothing. He needs you, Hugh."

"Rhys wouldn't lift a finger for me."

"You don't know that."

"Yes, I do. Besides, look where helping him got me. Another arrow wound and a dead—" He couldn't finish.

"What's the matter with you?" she snapped. "You can't believe the things you're saying."

It was as if he turned to stone then, his face hardening, his eyes cold. It wasn't Hugh in front of her but a mask of him, and it unnerved her. It hurt to see him like that, hurt to watch her friend recede behind what he thought was safe. She had seen Hugh be brave, take risks before, and not just for Rhys, but for her too. Where was that Hugh now?

"I think you'd better go now," he said, turning away from her.

She put her hand like a claw on his shoulder and whirled him around. His blank face stunned her, and she lowered her fist when he asked, "What're you gonna do? Hit me?"

Her fist shook, and she realized it wouldn't do

any good. She could beat him senseless and he would still have that blank expression. "No," she growled, her low voice scaring even her, "I'm gonna do what you don't have the guts to do."

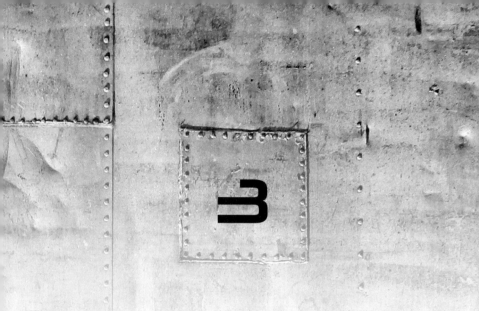

3

Hugh stopped when Colonel Klein's meaty hand landed on his shoulder. Suppressing his grimace, Hugh looked over at him.

"Remember, you got this visit on one condition." Klein leaned in, his eyes menacingly narrowed. "Make him understand."

Managing a nod, Hugh approached the cell block door once free of Klein's bearish grip. He was impatient to see Rhys, to ask how he was getting along after a week in prison. Klein's warning, however, dampened his spirits.

Rhys's bluff had been called. It turned out Hammond really couldn't afford the bad press incurred by keeping a thirteen-year-old in prison. Klein's decision not to beat Rhys like the others had spared her the worst of it, but there was general civilian unrest over so many being kept prisoner, especially someone so young.

To save face, the general granted Hugh a visit. There was a good deal of pomp and circumstance to go along with it—he had to go in mid-afternoon, when people would be out and about, able to see him going in. Hugh was told that, should he convince Rhys to sign a loyalty statement, which would go public, and tell Hammond what she wanted to know of the native capital, Rhys would walk out of prison that day.

Hugh had his doubts. He knew his brother was unlikely to give in, especially when he heard the terms. But it was a chance.

His footsteps echoed a little in the blindingly white corridor of the cell block as he walked to the second-to-last cell on the left. He caught the gaze of the native queen, in the last cell on the right, and swallowed hard.

"Hugh?"

He turned to find Rhys standing up off his cot to meet him.

"Hey," he said, "how're you doing?"

Rhys shrugged. "What're you doing here?"

"I came to see you."

"Well, yeah. Why'd they let you in?" His brother was suspicious, and he had reason to be.

Hugh cleared his throat. Leaning against the Plexiglas cell door, his back to the entrance, he said, "I'm here to talk to you."

Rhys's eyes narrowed. "About what?"

Though seven years older, Hugh found himself feeling inferior to Rhys. His nerve almost broke under that imperious scowl, and suddenly he felt like a scared little kid, ready to do whatever Rhys told him.

But right now he had to do what the colonel told him, even if, deep down, he knew it was wrong. He had to try and help Rhys.

"They might let you out," he said, "as early as today. All you need to do is sign a loyalty statement and answer a few questions. Then you're free to go. It isn't asking that much." The words felt slimy coming out of his mouth, and he worried he didn't sound convincing.

"Like hell," Rhys said through gritted teeth.

"You don't have to mean it," Hugh said as quietly as he could. "Just sign and get outta here."

Rhys's head shot up, and he glared at Hugh. "This's low, doing their dirty work."

"Rhys, I'm trying to help you. You've already spent all winter in *their* prison," he nodded at the native queen, "do you really want to spend more time here?"

"*They* treated me a lot better," Rhys growled. "I know what you're trying to do, Hugh, and it's not going to work. I'm not giving in to her like you obviously have."

Hugh's gut clenched. "Rhys, I'm just trying to do what's best for us. I'm trying to keep you safe."

"How many times do I have to tell you, you don't have to! I can take care of myself."

"And look where that's got you!"

Rhys winced as if the words stung him, and Hugh hoped his forcefulness might actually sway him. His hope dissipated like smoke in the wind as he watched Rhys's face harden. Hugh could see the thoughts whirring in his brother's head, his resolve solidifying, and Hugh knew he had lost.

"Look, I appreciate that you're trying to get me out." Rhys pressed up against the door too, saying quietly, "Just stay out of this, okay? I don't want you to get hurt again. I have to fight my own battles."

Hugh's forehead slumped against the door. "I can't talk you out of it?"

Rhys's eyes flicked up to Hugh. "You could help me. Really help me."

"Yes," almost sprang to Hugh's lips, but he couldn't get it out. Fear of the colonel, standing right outside, coiled around his heart, and he knew he couldn't do what Rhys asked. He didn't know if he wanted to. Hugh wanted a quiet life; he wanted to work and settle down and be at peace. There had been enough fighting, enough dying.

"I just hate seeing you in here," he said. He watched the mysterious and sudden fire in Rhys's eyes die.

Rhys nodded. "I won't be here forever."

"I'll be there when you get out."

They stood there, on opposite sides of the door, looking at anything but the other. Hugh didn't want to leave like this. He had let himself hope Rhys would be walking out with him, and the absurdity of that hope left him feeling hollow. He had lost his mentor, and now it felt like he had lost his brother. Again.

"Take care of yourself."

"You too," Rhys said, shoving his hands in his pockets.

Hugh turned to go but couldn't seem to move

any further. Over his shoulder he locked eyes with the native queen.

Walking past Rhys's inquisitive stare, Hugh went to stand before the last cell. The queen sat on the ground right on the other side of the door, watching him. Her ovular head, supported on a long, thin neck, rested against the wall, her square eyes with light blue irises angled up. Her nostrils flared a little when he squatted down.

Her iridescent skin rippled into several vibrant colors before settling back into a dark purple. They stared at one another for a long moment.

Tapping on his gauntlet, Hugh opened the translator program. He had had one installed for when he went south with a whole delegation to see the Tikshi people, a rival of the Charneki.

He knew he would probably get in trouble for it, but he had something to say.

"You don't know me," he said into the gauntlet, his words coming out as foreign, monotone syllables, "but I'm the one who killed your brother."

He watched as her color dipped into a deep blue. It hurt him too to recall that night. It had been dark. He just wanted to help Rhys. He saw natives coming at him, shot blindly, and hit the smaller one. It took a while to learn that not only had the young one been Rhys's friend, but also the brother of the queen.

"I'm sorry for it," he continued. "I wish I could go back and undo it. But I think we're even now. You've taken my brother from me." He glanced over his shoulder, saw Rhys with a baffled expression. "I'm not angry with you—but I would ask something, if it's all right."

He waited to see her reaction to the whole translation. Despite trying to keep her composure, the ends of her lipless mouth were downturned, the bottom lip quivering. To Hugh's surprise, she nodded.

"I want you to take care of him, because I can't."

The queen searched his face as the translation finished. He had expected more reaction from her and felt almost nervous as he waited for something.

Her nostrils flared again when she looked past Hugh at Rhys. When she spoke, her words were soft, and Hugh thought the translation didn't do her justice.

"He is Charneki now, and Charneki take care of their own."

Fighting tears, Hugh nodded and stood. "Thank you."

He lingered only a moment longer, all at once sore and grateful. The queen touched her hand to her head then held it out in front of her. Hugh nodded again.

When he walked past Rhys, he tried to grin.

Rhys blinked, his cheeks flushed.

"I'll see you later," Hugh said.

Walking out, Hugh found Colonel Klein not far from the entrance, his arms crossed.

"You've got some nerve."

Hugh shrugged, suddenly feeling numb about the whole endeavor. "He wouldn't agree. I thought maybe the queen could convince him."

Klein's eyes narrowed, but he let Hugh pass, following him out.

Hugh couldn't quite believe he had gotten out with barely a smack on the wrist, but he supposed him going to the prison so publicly was working in his favor. As high profile as Rhys was now, Hugh guessed he was too. At least for now. Whatever got Hugh home sooner.

"Straight to work," Klein said. "And keep quiet."

Hugh watched him stalk off with three of his soldiers towards the military quadrant. As he did, Hugh mused how he didn't want to go to work—at least not the work General Hammond had given him and an engineering team. She wanted a weapon of mass destruction and had only been deterred from making a nuclear weapon out of one of the generators—repurposed starship engines—by Saranov. They honestly could have been done by now, with all the hands, but the team worked as slowly as possible, hoping another solution would present itself before Hammond got a chance to use the weapon. Saranov's death slowed things further.

Shoving his hands in his pockets, Hugh turned towards the industrial quadrant. He stopped short when he saw Elena.

She walked towards him with a determined gait. Ulysses Carter, his hands cuffed behind his back, and another soldier, were in front of her.

He thought perhaps she was on-duty now as a prison guard, but something made him suspect.

"You'd better keep walking," she said after Carter and the other soldier passed.

"Be careful," he said.

She flashed him a quick grin. "Always am."

———

Rhys sat against the wall wondering what they had done to Hugh. His brother had always been the more timid of the twins, less inclined to fight, but Rhys had held out hope, even a little, that Hugh might come back to him. It was more than Rhys wanting to be the boss of Hugh again—he truly did wish he and his brother could agree on something.

Hugh always claimed he wanted to be brothers again, to make things like they were before, but Rhys knew he couldn't do this while Hugh opposed, or at least ambivalently stood against everything Rhys believed in.

Rhys's head drew up, and he moved so that he could look back at the cell block door. He frowned.

The door slid open to reveal Ulysses Carter being led by two soldiers. Rhys's heart sank. Carter's luck of getting out of prison within a few days wouldn't hold true this time. Hammond wouldn't let him out of her sight.

As the first soldier started tapping on a cell's command monitor, the second one eased behind him. Rhys's eyebrows shot up. Elena?

In one fluid movement, she raised her arm and brought it down on the base of the soldier's neck.

He yelped, crumpling, and with another blow to the head, he was out. It took her only another moment to free Carter of his cuffs and then she was stalking down the corridor.

Decked in full military uniform, she had a rifle slung across her back and two handguns strapped in holsters around her hips. Her left sleeve was pulled up, leaving her gauntlet free, and a small device rested in her ear.

"I'm in," she said, striding towards him. "I need these cells open."

Rhys heard Cass's faint voice say, "Gimme two seconds," from the comlink in Elena's ear.

He looked up at Elena. "What're you doing here?"

She gave him a look. "What's it look like? Prison break."

A mechanical *click* forced his door open two inches.

Elena wrapped her fingers through the opening and began pulling. She strained, the automechanism apparently disabled. Carter came jogging up and, after giving Rhys a wink, helped create a big enough space for Rhys to step out.

"Second one now."

They made quicker work of this one, and the queen's slim frame slipped through. The queen looked down upon them with wide eyes.

"What is happening, Rhys?" she asked.

"We are running away," he said.

A small smile spread over her face.

They started back down the cell block, but Rhys couldn't help asking, "What about the others?"

"No time," Elena said. "It's gonna be hard enough breaking you two out."

Casting a guilty look back into the prison, he caught Jana's gaze, and she nodded at him.

The front room of the prison was a cacophony of sounds and movement, five soldiers readying for battle. The instant the door slid open, Elena unleashed a bout of gunfire, covering their retreat to the desk, where Carter disabled the guard.

Handing Carter one of her handguns, they sped through the firefight that broke out.

Rhys and the queen crouched behind them, their hands plastered over their ears. They exchanged looks.

Elena took the last shot, firing at a soldier's plated vest, knocking them back into a set of lockers. Carter covered her as she ran up, disarmed him, and left him unconscious.

"No!"

Rushing back to the control panel on the main desk, she tried to override the entrance's riot door.

"Any time now, Cass!" she roared into the earpiece.

"Go, go, I'll hold it!"

Cass kept it open just long enough—Carter's jacket hem almost caught in the closing doors as they flew past and hurried out into the afternoon.

They could hear gunshots but none were aimed at them, and Elena urged them to hurry from the building and down the slight slope away from the hilltop where the prison stood. The firefight they heard was taking place about three hundred yards away where thirty members of the resistance were fending off a unit of soldiers.

"This's where I leave you kids," said Carter, flashing them a smile. "We'll hold 'em as long as we can."

"Don't get killed," Elena called after him.

Rhys's heart jumped into his throat watching Carter head for the fray while three more units sped towards them from the hangars. Elena saw it too and hurried them south, slightly to the left of the fray, and Rhys saw a cruiser waiting for them.

Breaking into a full run, they careened down the slope towards the cruiser. Glancing over his shoulder, Rhys saw that half a unit had broken off and was coming for them now.

"Cass, how's that virus coming?" Elena said, her voice tense as she aimed a few shots behind them.

"Could be better."

They heard cries to their right, and Rhys looked to see the resistance line caving, soldiers swarming around, and suddenly they made a break for the residential quadrant.

"Damn," Elena muttered.

"Will they be okay?"

Elena didn't answer; she kept urging him to go faster. The queen had an easy time keeping up with them and honestly could have been to the cruiser by now.

Suddenly Elena fell, and Rhys cried out. He skidded to a stop, saw soldiers coming at them; the ground that had been beneath Elena's foot wasn't there anymore.

She pushed him away when he came back for her. "Get to the cruiser!"

He helped her up nonetheless but started running for the vehicle after she pushed him again. He could hear her almost keeping up with them, her footsteps irregular.

"Get in, get in!" she cried.

Rhys ripped the passenger door open and motioned for the queen to get in. She leapt in with inhuman grace, and Rhys slammed the door shut. He clamored into the backseat, his breath coming in sporadic bursts.

Elena was backed up against the driver door, firing at the oncoming soldiers.

Pulling himself over the front seat, Rhys struggled for the latch. He had his fingertips on it, just couldn't get it. The queen reached over, wrapped her slim fingers around it instead.

"Push!" he said.

The door flung open, and Rhys yelled, "C'mon, get in!"

Elena made for the opening but slammed against the back passenger door, hit in the shoulder. She grunted in pain, then held up her good arm with the handgun shakily.

He got a hand on her unhurt upper arm and started pulling. He and the queen cried out when a shot hit the middle of the front seat.

The queen leaned over and pulled Elena up into the driver's seat and reached for the door handle.

"Watch out!"

The door slammed just in time to block a volley of gunshots.

"Thanks," Elena said breathlessly, bringing the cruiser to life and slamming on the gas.

Thrown back, it took Rhys a moment to regain his balance. They bounced around in the cab, Elena not sticking to the roads, instead veering this way and that to avoid taking more damage.

Pressed up against the window, Rhys's eyes went wide as they sped past Hugh, who was walking towards the industrial quadrant. The brothers locked gazes, and then Hugh was gone.

"What about now?" Elena barked into her comlink.

"Just another minute!"

"You don't have a minute! I can see the damn thing!"

Rhys's throat caught when he saw the perimeter

looming up ahead of them. It glowed light blue. Armed, it could electrocute them in two seconds flat.

"No, no, no!" Cass chanted on the other end.

"*Cass!*"

Swerving, Elena narrowly avoided ramming the perimeter, instead drove along parallel.

"I'm in! Hang on, I almost . . . "

"We need it *now*!"

A contingent of speeders now made towards them from the northeast, and soon they wouldn't have any lead, not to mention a way to escape.

"You're good!"

Rhys slammed against the window as Elena jerked the steering wheel, the cruiser crunching untouched terrain under its wheels.

"We're out!"

"That wasn't so hard."

Elena scoffed.

"Take care of yourself, okay?"

"Yeah. You too." Elena's voice sounded full.

"Cutting transmission."

Pulling the comlink out of her ear, Elena wrapped both hands around the steering wheel.

Rhys knew they still had to outrun the speeders, but he felt almost buoyant. She had done it.

"That does not look good," the queen said, bringing Rhys back.

He pulled himself forward so he could look over the front seat at Elena. Her shoulder was indeed oozing blood from a circular wound that looked like a small open mouth.

"There should be a med-pack under the back-seat," she said through a grimace.

Easing himself into the leg space between the front and back seats, Rhys felt around in the relative dark until his hand hit a box.

"Got it!"

Sitting up, he yanked open the box and set upon the supplies, ripping open a packet of gauze. He leaned forward again and opened a tube of antibacterial and anti-inflammatory paste. Rubbing this onto the wound with a light hand and some gauze, he then packed the wound over with bandage.

Elena let him do it, her teeth clenched, as she sped southwest.

"Are you gonna be okay the rest of the way?" he asked. They both knew from experience that the journey could take upwards of five days.

She gave him a hard look. "Hell yeah."

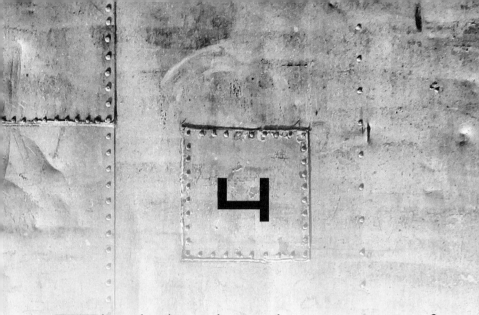

4

Though she only caught rare snippets of what they said, Zeneba couldn't help being amused by the two humans. They were arguing again; despite being wounded, the female, Elena, refused to give up driving the vehicle. Zeneba shared Rhys's opinion that perhaps he should take over driving, if only to give Elena a rest, but she remained obstinate.

Rhys seemed to be fighting for his cause one last time, for they were nearing Karak, the Charneki's beautiful mountain-city. Zeneba could barely contain how relieved she was to be nearing her home.

She was, however, struggling against some small

trepidation. She didn't know who she would be returning to—the battle had claimed so many. Would Ondra be waiting for her? Yaro?

Zeneba looked at Rhys when she realized their talking had ceased. He had a gruff look about him, and Zeneba smiled when he looked at her.

"She is stubborn like the *unmala*," she said.

He nodded in agreement.

Elena said something, and Rhys pulled himself up against their front seats.

"We are almost there," he said.

Zeneba let the golden pleasure show on her skin, and she turned her head to watch the top of her palace come into view. She felt weightless, her innards tied in knots, as the city grew above them.

Coming to a stop on the eastern bluffs overlooking the bay, Zeneba's breath escaped her as she looked down upon her home. It was all there, just as she had left it. Banners flapped in the afternoon breeze. The calm surface of the bay shimmered, reflecting an almost clear sky. And her city, with her palace and the Red Hall, where her throne stood, at the very top, stood waiting for her.

Tears sprung to her eyes, and she looked over at Elena. Gently, she touched the human's forearm.

"Thank you," she said. "Your courage means so much to me. Charneki will sing your praises for a thousand cycles."

Elena's eyes went wide at her words after they were translated. Clearing her throat, she nodded, easing the cruiser back into motion.

"Make for Oria," Zeneba directed, pointing at the city along the sandy southern coast of the bay. "Once there we can find a boat to take us across."

"Why wait for a boat?" Elena said, her words turned into monotone Charneki. "I can do better."

Zeneba's mouth hung open slightly, unsure what to say to that, and she glanced back at Rhys. He just shrugged. It seemed pointless to argue with the determined glint in Elena's eye.

Speeding down towards Oria, Zeneba could soon see Charneki emerging from their halls, some having caught sight of the human vehicle making its way towards them.

Elena didn't wait for them, taking directions from Zeneba to the docks. They sped past dumbfounded, fearful faces, and Zeneba realized that her people didn't know what to think of the spectacle. She hadn't time to say anything, however, before Elena had them flying for the water.

"Wait, we'll fall in!"

Clasping her hands on either side of her face, Zeneba winced as the vehicle went sailing through the air, Elena making rapid little movements on the device screen next to the vehicle's steering wheel.

Daring to look out her window, Zeneba's mouth fell open when she saw the vehicle was afloat. Elena eased it forward through the water, plying the waves.

Elena grinned when she saw Zeneba's astonished face.

As they passed through the harbor gate, she

saw a nervous crowd already gathered. Turning to Elena, she said, "Please, my people must see me."

Nodding, Elena touched another button and then pointed up.

Following with her eyes, Zeneba saw that the window on the roof was opening. Thanking Elena, she pulled her upper half up into the sunlight and balanced on her seat.

The vehicle came out of the water onto Karak before those amassed quite knew what was happening. Once they saw their *mara*, however, their skin turned light yellow with surprise, but quickly rippled into a deep gold.

"Hang on up there," she heard Elena say, and then they were moving up the main promenade, towards the palace.

Zeneba beamed to see her people, now streaming from their halls and workshops to see her. Great cheers and sounds of relief rang out, and she returned their joy with her golden hue and smile. She was home.

The ride up to the palace was the quickest Zeneba had ever taken, and soon she saw the palace walls' facade, adorned with statues of her predecessors. The great jade and iron gates stood open, beckoning her.

Elena stopped at the foot of the great staircase which led directly up to the Red Hall, from which her turquoise-robed Elders came rushing.

Turning back to the crowd of Charneki standing just behind, she said, "Nahara has blessed us today. Words cannot express how happy I am to be home."

They cried blessings for her and gave thanks to their beloved suns for her safe return.

Slipping back down into the vehicle, she said to Elena and Rhys, "Come with me."

The three of them stepped out of the vehicle and started up the stairs to meet the group hurrying to them.

Zeneba smiled to see the big Charneki in the lead, and she ran to meet Yaro. Ignoring propriety, she threw her arms around the Head of her Guard.

To her surprise Yaro caught her up in his arms and held her tight. When she looked upon him her eyes went wide to see small tears running down his face. She wiped them away, smiling at him.

"I'm home, Yaro."

He smiled through his tears. "I have missed you so."

"I've missed you too."

"But how are you here? I thought . . . "

Taking a step back, she held her hand out to Rhys and Elena. "They brought me back."

Yaro smiled to see the two humans. She knew he was fond of Rhys from his time in Karak, and Zeneba always suspected he liked Elena, for when it had been him in that human cell, she had been kind to him.

"All of us thank you," he said. "We can never repay this debt."

Placing his left hand on his right shoulder, Yaro bowed his head. The Elders behind him did too, and when she looked down upon those of Karak, she saw a wave of bowing heads.

Elena and Rhys looked overwhelmed and rather embarrassed.

"It is as I said. We shall sing your praises for a thousand cycles." Smiling down at them, she ushered them further up the stairs, greeting Elders as she went.

When she came to the top, she took the outstretched hands of Elder Zhora. His sightless, milky eyes were glassy.

"Nahara has answered my prayers," he said.

"It is good to see you, Skywatcher. I have been away far too long."

He squeezed her hands. "You are here now, and you make your people happy. You give them much needed hope."

She turned back towards the crowd and another cheer rang out when they saw their *mara* at the mouth of the Red Hall, about to sit once more upon her seat. She thrust her fist into the air, and a sea of golden celebration answered her.

She made to move into the Hall but almost

stumbled. Putting a hand to her side, she held in her grimace. She couldn't hide her pain from Yaro, though.

"Please, Golden One, you must see a healer."

"In good time," she said, straightening. "First I must hear all that you can tell me."

As she walked into the Red Hall, the host of Elders and Chieftains following her, Zeneba tried not to dwell on the face she hadn't seen.

Her seat, carved from the topmost stone of Karak, stood across the Hall from her, and she strode towards it, ignoring the aching throb in her side. When she reached it, she turned and sat.

"It fills us with joy to see you sitting there again," said Elder Plia.

"Thank you, Wise One. While in the human prison I thought of nothing else but returning home."

"Were those demons cruel to you?" asked Elder Ha.

Her upper lip twitched. "The humans are indeed

77

ruled by a vicious *mara* who yearns for more war. Her heart is sick. But there are some," she said, looking down upon Rhys and Elena, "who are brave enough to stand against her."

"Please, Golden One," said Chieftain Ura, stepping forward. "We must tell you that the Tikshi are headed north by sea."

Zeneba's gut clenched. The Tikshi had been enemies of the Charneki since ancient times. Yalah, the first *mar*, had banished them across the treacherous waters of Umarr's Finger to their jungle island. Ever since, the Tikshi had been trying to fight their way to a foothold on Charnek.

"How far are they?"

"Our last report this morning said two hundred leagues."

She swallowed hard, then nodded. "Are defensive measures already in place?"

"Yes, Golden One. The army has not been dismissed and is awaiting your orders."

"We suspect they will try for a night raid," said Chieftain Heta. Zeneba was relieved to see her relatively unharmed as well.

"We should be ready for them, though," said Elder Jeska. He looked up at her and smiled. "Your project had foresight, Golden One. We shall be attaching the *generators* to the *spotlights* tonight."

Zeneba smiled down at Rhys when she heard the human words come from Elder Jeska. Before riding off to battle, Zeneba had worked with Rhys and the other humans kept in Karak to make what the humans called generators. Used to make light, upon their initial success, Zeneba had won enough support for her project to have the humans make more generators to power great lights that they would use to watch the coastline for an incoming attack.

"I am pleased to hear this. We will take away their advantage."

"There is more, Golden One."

Looking upon Chieftain Samuka of the southern coasts, she bade him speak.

"As you know, the Tikshi entered into an alliance with the humans not long ago. If the Tikshi move to attack us now, the humans cannot be far behind."

"Are we ready for two waves of attack?" she asked.

"Reinforcements have been called upon from every corner of the Marland," Yaro said.

"Will they be here in time?"

Yaro's mouth was a grim line.

Zeneba took a breath. "Karak has never fallen before. We will all stand like mountains."

Those in the Hall cried out their agreement.

Taking a step forward, Rhys said, "*Mara*, may I speak?"

"Yes, Rhys. We will listen."

Looking hesitantly at the others over his shoulder, he said, "We may be able to do something about the humans."

"Like what?"

"We might try and stop them before they can come to Karak."

"You want us to ride north again?" Chieftain Heta demanded.

He shook his head. "No. I mean to say that we might ask other humans to stop them."

They looked surprised at him. "There are more who resist your *mara*?" asked Elder Plia.

"Many more."

"And you could speak with these others?" Zeneba asked.

He nodded. "We could try."

She smiled. "You would have my thanks, little one. Please, see what can be done."

Rhys bowed his head.

Looking out at all of them gathered before her, Zeneba said, "A time of trial comes. Let us meet it. Please, make safe our city."

They bowed to her, and with a few more words of thanks and relief, they disbanded to see to their tasks. As the last of them left the Red Hall, she looked down at Rhys and Elena.

She frowned to see Rhys supporting Elena, the female looking pale despite her dark skin. The bandage she wore over her hurt shoulder was red with human blood.

"We must get her to a healer," she said, stepping down from her seat. Clapping her hands once, an attendant rushed to them from a hidden side door. "Quickly, take them to see Healer Puna. And bring one of their humans to see her."

Bowing her head, the attendant urged Rhys and Elena to follow her.

Zeneba nodded at Rhys when he looked at her. "We'll speak later."

A small grin spread across his face. "I am happy to see you returned."

"I have you to thank."

As she watched the humans follow the attendant out, Yaro came up beside her.

"You should see the healer as well," he said.

She knew he spoke sense, and she yearned for a numbing salve for her side, but there was something she had to do first.

"Yaro, be truthful with me. Did . . . did Ondra return with you?" She held her breath as she awaited his answer.

"Yes, Golden One. But he was badly wounded."

She felt a surge of relief and dread. "How badly?"

"Shall I take you to him?"

"Please."

Nodding, Yaro led her from the Hall, down to the second tier, and then headed around to the south face of the palace, catching a smaller staircase down into the Guard's section. She tried not to think too much about his not answering her directly as she followed.

As they walked past those of her Guard, she nodded at each of the warriors who stopped in surprise and saluted her.

Yaro brought her to a small room steeped in soft blue light by burning *buna* lamps. Taking a step in, she saw Ondra laid out on a narrow bed, his eyes closed, his chest rising and falling steadily.

"The healer said his body is weak. But I know his spirit is strong. Seeing you should strengthen him."

"Thank you, Yaro," she said, tears already welling in her eyes.

"I will be right outside if you need me."

Nodding but not really hearing him, Zeneba took the three steps towards Ondra in a sort of daze. A ghastly cut ran over his right eye, starting along his forehead and running all the way down to the jaw, splitting one of his swirls of iridescent skin. The cut-off section of skin had already turned black. A circular wound framed in fading bruises adorned his chest, and Zeneba realized with a pang that he had taken a shot from a human weapon. Her tears spilled over when she thought how his armor had barely saved him.

Kneeling down beside his bed, she touched a hand to his head.

His eyes opened slowly at the touch, and he blinked several times before he looked at her. It seemed he couldn't comprehend what he saw, for he stared at her as if she were an apparition.

"I've come home, love," she said softly.

His mouth opened, and a frown shadowed his eyes. "I dream again."

"No," she shook her head, "no, I've come back to you." She took his hand in hers and held it against her forehead.

His nostrils flared and tears began to run down his cheeks. "Th-they took you."

"Yes."

His skin rippled into a deep blue. "I-I couldn't get to you."

"Shh, it's all right. There was nothing you could do. But I'm here now." She pressed her head against his.

She felt his hand, lightly at first, rest against the

side of her head, and the hand she held between her own squeezed. He said her name, and her heart stung. Her separation from him had been the hardest, but seeing him lying there was almost worse. She wrapped an arm around him, and they wept together.

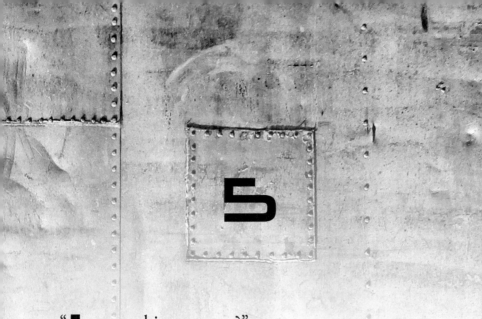

5

"**I**s something wrong?"

Cass looked, startled, over her shoulder at Hugh's question.

He tried to smile but found her wide-eyed expression disconcerting. He frowned.

Backing away from the weapon, which stood with all its wiring and activation monitor in the center of the warehouse, Cass smiled at him, but it didn't reach her eyes. Part of the design team, rather than the engineering team, there wasn't a reason for her to be looking it over like she was.

"Just looking everything over."

They both knew she was lying. Guessing by Elena's recent team-up with the resistance to break Rhys and the native queen out of prison, Hugh suspected Cass was part of the resistance too. Never one to stifle her beliefs, Cass certainly seemed the type to join.

But why wasn't she with them now? After the prison break, the resistance holed itself up in the southern sector of the residential quadrant. Forming a barricade, they were holding their ground against Hammond's troops. Most found it amazing they had held out so long—it helped that the resistance had gotten their hands on grade-A weapons and even a few armed cruisers, thanks to Elena's mentor Sgt. White, who now led the resistance with Carter. Hammond wasn't able to spare all her resources for this urban warfare. She was preparing for a strike against the natives.

A line in the sand had been drawn, and no civilian could ignore it, not when their homes were now in the direct line of fire. Many had stopped going to work. Some had crossed the barricade and joined the resistance, while others enlisted with Hammond. New Haven was splintering.

Hugh realized that perhaps Cass's position on the outside was too important for her to join the ranks. He glanced at the weapon behind her and wondered if she had truly been able to sabotage it. Sabotage had been a whispered suggestion since the beginning, but Saranov himself had quashed this, saying it was too risky. Hugh now knew why.

He returned her half-hearted smile, and they joined the others of the team to await Hammond's last inspection. They weren't quite done with the weapon yet—a few calibrations were still in order—but she would be leaving on campaign any day now.

"Can you believe it's come to this?" she whispered to him.

"It's out of our hands now."

She made a face. "Not yet."

Hugh remained silent, not wanting to betray what he really thought. Some part of him dearly hoped she had been able to sabotage the weapon. He knew that Rhys was in the native city, the place where Hammond would wage her war.

Still, though, he couldn't bring himself to help. He hoped Cass had succeeded but knew, if she hadn't, that he wouldn't do it. It nagged at him, this ever-increasing hesitation. He was scared of everything. Rhys wasn't even in New Haven to threaten, but he didn't think himself strong enough to do what he knew was right. He might break if he tried.

General Hammond didn't keep them waiting long. Striding in with an armed escort behind her, she placed herself feet away from the weapon and folded her hands behind her back.

"Good morning," she said. When she didn't get an answer, she continued, "I'm pleased with the progress you've made. I hope to never have to use this weapon, but I sleep better at night knowing we have this trick up our sleeve. Preparations are underway and by tomorrow, I will be leading our forces to the enemy stronghold to fight for your freedom."

He felt Cass shift slightly beside him and prayed she wouldn't say anything.

"I expect you to work hard in my absence. I'm leaving behind a unit of my personal bodyguards to help you with whatever you need."

Hugh looked over at the stone-faced watchdogs, knowing exactly who it was they would really be helping.

"I know not all of you have supported this project. However, I want to stress that if it comes to it, this may be humanity's last defense. We must show these natives that we're here to stay, and if we have to drop this on them, well, then, I daresay they'll think twice before threatening us again."

Though he couldn't quite figure out why Hammond wanted to go to battle rather than wait for the weapon to be finished, he wasn't complaining.

He supposed she couldn't, at this point, risk such blatant genocide, not with a civil war on her hands. If things went south, as she said, the weapon would become a godsend rather than what it really was.

For now she stuck to traditional warfare, and Hugh felt that some part of the general preferred it this way. Good, old fashioned killing. They had already melted down what Hammond deemed unnecessary buildings for the metal, to replace what material had been irreparably damaged in the Battle of San Angelo. And now she was ready.

"We're going to war hopefully for the last time. When I return, we'll put all of this civil strife nonsense to rest and get on with peaceful, prosperous lives. But for now we must fight for that future and claim Terra Nova for our own."

She looked out at them with a smug face, but suddenly that fell away as a voice came over her comlink earpiece. Hugh couldn't hear what it said, but it seemed to shock the general, and she whirled on her heels, making her way quickly back out of the building.

"What d'you mean *now*? They're not supposed to be there for three days . . . "

———————

The horns came like a cry in the night, but Zeneba hadn't been asleep. Lifting her head, she gazed out over the terrace, her eyes fixed on the narrow opening of the bay. Great balls of white light shone down upon the churning surface, illuminating the first of the Tikshi warships.

She sensed rather than saw Yaro come up behind her. "Prepare for battle," she said.

He was away in a moment, and she made to follow him more slowly, her side still not allowing free movement. She paused only long enough to lay a hand on the smooth jade face of her brother Zaynab. In effigy, he looked asleep with the inkiness of night blanketing him.

"Bless me, little brother."

Her crimson robes billowed about her in the cool night breeze as she strode from Zaynab's monument. The upper half of the robe was secured beneath a gleaming cuirass, Nahara and Undin cresting over Karak etched along the breast face, and shoulder plates curled over her upper chest like wings. The sleeves padded her skin against the gauntlets she wore, metal imitations of the *lahn-nahar*, her royal vestments. When she reached the main staircase, she placed her golden helmet, made especially for her to fit her unique headdress, a natural crown of skin and bone that female Charneki grew, upon her head.

Below her, the mountain was alive with light. Wood and *buna* torches clashed to make red, blue, purple light snaking through all the tiers of the city, and the bright white of the spotlights, mounted at the opening of the bay and along the rim, swung about to reveal the forming flotilla.

Her Guard amassed at her back, and Yaro made

his way up the stairs quickly to her. Bowing his head, he stood beside her.

"Everyone is behind the market wall?"

He nodded. "The people have been moved back and are taking shelter in homes. Your warriors stand ready at the harbor wall."

She swallowed hard. That was where this campaign would be decided: the harbor. Karak had three series of walls, the first sitting around the base of Karak like a ring, the mouth of which formed the harbor. The gates had been closed with Charneki regiments amassing behind it. Those on foot stood along the shallow steps leading out of the water, and those on *garans* floated just behind the gate. More soldiers stood atop the harbor wall, arrows notched, awaiting her command.

The harbor wall was sturdy, but should they be forced back, the Tikshi would have to contend with the market wall, even higher, though less thick, and they would be without their boats. The palace wall was the last of the three, and no enemy had ever reached it.

In the illumination of the spotlight, she caught a branch of the flotilla breaking off and said, "Warn Oria."

A warrior to her left nodded and put his lips to a smaller horn, which released a low sound. A moment later one of Karak's horns bellowed, warning its sister across the bay.

Zeneba tried to take a nervous breath, but it caught in her throat. She doubted she would ever get used to battle, though this time she would be more of a spectator than participant. It was tradition that a *mar* or *mara* be before the Red Hall should Karak come under siege, but having led her army against the human colony herself, Zeneba felt a twinge of guilt for standing at the top of the mountain when the danger was far below.

"You must trust your warriors," Yaro had said. "They fight for you."

"I wish I were fighting for them."

But neither Yaro nor her council would hear of it. She was only just returned and still healing. The Charneki could not bear to lose their *mara* again.

The bay was a terrible sight, the water barely visible as more and more Tikshi ships flooded in. They made as one for Karak and would crash down on them like a wave in a few moments. Waiting for this in silence was torturous.

Another of Karak's horns sounded, and along the outside eastern and western stretches of the harbor wall emerged hundreds of Charneki warriors atop *garans* from the water. Dripping wet, their weapons gleamed as a great cry went out. Zeneba winced when the first wave of them hit the front ships.

Wood cracking, metal clashing, it was all terrible noise. Her heart beat painfully and irregularly as she watched.

Despite the amphibian companies, waves of

Tikshi ships rammed the harbor wall. Under heavy fire from the archers atop the wall, the Tikshi began mounting the gate, using ropes and thick cut ladders to scale up. Her breath caught when the first few Tikshi reached the top of the wall.

Yaro put his own horn to his mouth and let loose the fine timbre. All archers who could dipped their arrows into a *buna* flame and set these sailing into the flotilla. Ships sizzled like *su'ya* scales in the sun, a terrible hiss reverberating along the water.

Zeneba dared to think, if only for a moment, that perhaps this wouldn't be as bad as she thought. Then she looked along the northern rim of the bay, just west of the mouth, and saw torchlight being waved about frantically. She put a hand on Yaro's forearm.

Seeing it too, he grabbed up another horn from the warrior beside him and pointed it towards the cliffs. He received back two quick bouts.

"There are more scaling the cliffs. They will occupy our reinforcements."

Zeneba nodded stiffly. "Then we must hold them."

She had been counting on the forces along the northern cliffs to mop up the flotilla once the army in Karak routed it. With the troops on the cliffs preoccupied, the Tikshi might rally, away from the city, and launch a second attack. She could hardly discern anything from so far away, but clashing silhouettes against bright orange flame worried her.

With another blow from Yaro's first horn, the archers redoubled their efforts and the regiments just inside the harbor wall readied. She could see Tikshi jumping down into the water; her warriors were ready for them.

A groan that shook the whole mountain came from the gate. The iron sounded like a wounded animal, bending and breaking as chains pulled it back. Great hooks gripped the gate like talons, and hundreds of Tikshi oarsmen worked to open it.

"Get everyone back," she said quickly, "either into the palace or underground!"

A high-pitched horn sounded, and Zeneba watched, her stomach in knots, as Charneki streamed from their halls up the slope to the palace. Those who were furthest from the palace wall made for the nearest tunnel opening into the mountain, knowing Karak had always shielded them in the past.

With a deafening *crack* the harbor gate opened, and Tikshi streamed into Karak. There were Charneki blades to meet them. Lines broke down, giving way to chaotic, bloody fighting in alleys and shops.

She couldn't help clutching at Yaro's arm.

He looked down at her. "We will protect you, Golden One."

"I'm not worried about myself," she said, unable to look away.

Suddenly she worried about the countless wounded in Karak. If the worst should happen, how would they get them out? Ondra? She would carry him herself if she had to.

The fighting lasted all through the night, and a red dawn rose, streaks of smoke blocking out Nahara and Undin. The Tikshi came with all their hatred, all their ambition, and they cut down many Charneki warriors. But they did not reach the market wall.

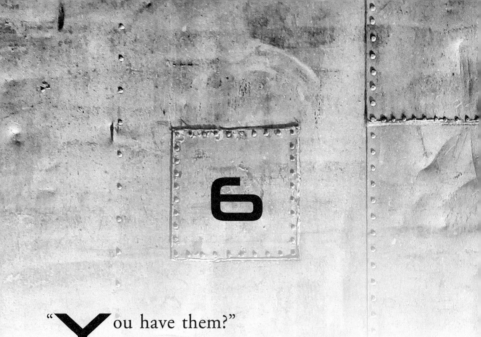

6

"**Y**ou have them?"

"Yes, Golden One, they survived and have been found."

Nodding, Zeneba said to Yaro, "Take me to them."

Yaro bowed his head and started down the main promenade from the market wall.

Zeneba followed him, glancing at the wall that had not wavered in its defense. The baked red stone filled her with pride, but her eyes stung with tiredness. So much had happened; so much still to do.

As she and Yaro walked, she met the eyes of those who looked upon her. She tried to be comforting, reassuring, but understood the forlorn glint in her peoples' eyes. All along the road, in alleyways, spilling out of private halls were bodies. Some were still alive, tended to by their families or munificent strangers. The healers of Karak and Oria were hard-pressed, and more had been sent for from the surrounding villages.

So many had been wounded or killed. Zeneba could hardly stomach it. She hadn't had to witness the aftermath of her previous battles; she had been spirited away from both. Now she saw the terrible price her people paid, and it made her never want to go to war again.

There were Tikshi bodies too, but these lay unattended in the sun.

Zeneba followed Yaro to the harbor where the Tikshi captives were. Most were from the ships in the rear of the fleet and had barely seen battle before the Charneki decimated their lines. There were over a thousand; many had been subdued on their ships.

The air was spicy with smoke, plumes billowing from the northern cliffs. The Charneki, under Chieftains Heta and Ura, had just barely defeated those Tikshi who scaled the cliffs, and now their bodies were burning in piles. From Chieftain Heta's account, it had been a hard victory, more than half of her forces gone. They had been caught off guard, a fact that seemed to gnaw at the proud Heta.

"Is it true, then, Yaro?" she asked as they neared the harbor.

There was more activity down here, warriors moving about, helping the wounded, working on fixing the harbor gate.

"Yes, Golden One. Vasya betrayed us."

As they came upon a small group of Tikshi captives, mostly generals, Zeneba told herself to keep her emotions in check.

She didn't want to believe Vasya had sided with the Tikshi, but it hadn't surprised her. Formerly Elder Vasya, the Charneki had been one of

Zeneba's tutors and a member of her council. He had never supported her. She had banished him from Karak, a decision Elder Zhora warned her would have consequences because of Vasya's pride. She hadn't imagined this would be his revenge.

As she and Yaro came upon the captives, several of her Chieftains met them, including Heta and Samuka.

Bowing to her, Chieftain Heta said, "We must deal with these *prrari* with an iron hand."

"What do you suggest?"

"They mustn't be allowed to strike us again."

Swallowing hard, Zeneba nodded. Her Chieftains parted for her as she walked up to the captives, bound and set in a row upon their knees. Most stared pointedly at the ground, save two.

"You should have known better, Vasya," she said.

His face remained frustratingly emotionless. Vasya searched her face, and Zeneba tried not to squirm. Her confidence crumbled around her, and she resented him for making her feel like a child again.

"I set out to prove what I have always said—you're a petulant child who cannot hope to lead them."

Zeneba's lip twitched.

"You will show respect," Yaro spat, "to the *mara*."

Vasya looked up and down the length of her. "She is not my *mara*."

Crossing her arms, Zeneba said, "I have survived your tests, all of them. I do not have to prove myself to a *prrari*."

Calling Vasya a traitor, a *prrari*, the highest insult a Charneki could wrap their tongue around, didn't come naturally. He was still Charneki. But he had betrayed his kind, had orchestrated the cliff attack, and this couldn't be forgiven.

Looking down at him with her head tilted up, Zeneba moved on to the only other face that would meet her gaze.

"This must be Treya."

She wasn't sure how much Charneki the Tikshi chieftain spoke, but she felt sure he understood her. His nostrils flared, and his eyes squinted slightly. One of his tusks had been broken off.

"Is it your curse, you Tikshi, to never be happy with what has been given you?"

"Stand there in your might," he growled in coarse Charneki. "But do not talk to me of curses. It is I who curse you."

Zeneba glared down at him. "You have lost, Treya. Curse me if you will, but it won't change that."

Turning his ugly head skyward, Treya laughed in the face of Nahara and Undin.

Zeneba slapped him across the face. "How dare you?"

"You should fear my curse, for I promise you shall feel what we Tikshi know well—you will lose." He leaned forward, his smile malicious. "Then you will have to be *happy* with what has been given you."

Zeneba tried to keep her heart from racing, his words making the blood in her veins pump rapidly. His words scared her, right down to her core, and he knew it.

Stepping forward, Yaro said, "Let us be done with them, Golden One."

Chieftain Heta nodded. "We could spill them into the sea. I doubt any can swim for long."

Zeneba's eyes flicked past the small group of captives, out onto the boats gently bobbing in the water. A thousand Tikshi sat on those decks. She swallowed hard. A thousand bodies, drowning in the sea.

She found she was shaking her head.

"Golden One?" Yaro asked.

"We could put them to the sword then," continued Chieftain Heta. "It will take longer, of course."

"No, Chieftain. There has been enough killing."

"Golden One, they attacked us. We must—"

"Chieftain. They have been defeated. A new treaty will be made up, and tribute will be paid."

The Chieftain scoffed, but Yaro glared at her.

"To do this, Golden One, makes it seem as if there are no consequences," said Chieftain Samuka finally.

"They will not all be sent back." She looked down at Vasya and Treya. "These two shall be put to death. In Treya's place, I shall appoint a new Tikshi chieftain."

The other Tikshi muttered once Zeneba's words were passed around.

"You would put a Charneki to death in place of a Tikshi?" Chieftain Heta said.

Zeneba's lip twitched. "He is no Charneki—nor is he Tikshi. He is *unvalah* and does not deserve mercy."

Turning from the harbor, she put a hand on Yaro's forearm and said, "See this done for me?"

"Of course, Golden One."

Nodding, she set her sights for the palace, with her Chieftains following. They had much to discuss; Karak needed to be made ready for the human attack they knew was coming. The question was when and how long Karak would give them.

"If you will have me slaughtered, you will look me in the eye!"

Zeneba looked over her shoulder to see Yaro forcing Vasya back down onto his knees.

"Or do you not have the stomach?"

"The last thing you shall see of this world is my back. It is all you deserve."

She told herself to keep moving, even as she heard slicing and two heavy, wet *thumps*. Feeling sick to her stomach, she focused on keeping one foot in front of the other.

She stopped, frowned when she heard a strange sound. It was distant, like an echo, and she looked across the bay, her eyes meeting the screams that flew across the water. Her eyes went wide. Oria was under attack.

Propping herself up onto her elbows, Elena frowned. Where those gunshots?

The others in the room looked about nervously. They had been in this room, a converted storeroom, for three days. Rhys told her this had been their room for some time; they moved out of the dungeons long ago. The human prisoners were treated well, given many amenities such as cushions and tables, and thanks to their success with the generator project, allowed a few freedoms.

Despite this, when the alarm was raised, the humans had been hustled into the storeroom, with guards posted outside. The queen had told them this would happen beforehand—she said it was for their safety. All of them knew, however, that the Charneki couldn't afford to have their prisoners turn on them if they were so inclined.

It didn't seem like any were, though. Elena had been surprised to see most of the former delegation working alongside Charneki. There were a few soldiers who refused to help, though, and they were probably the reason for the four guards outside.

Gingerly sitting up so as not to anger her wound too badly, Elena watched as Rhys pulled himself to the narrow slit window at the far side of the room. They all watched him, eager for news.

"What's going on?" asked Cara, one of scientists.

"I can't . . . " Rhys crammed his head further into the opening. "They're attacking—we are! We're already in the water!"

There was a scramble for the other two windows, faces pressing against the red stone. But while the others clamored for a look, Rhys backed away, turning towards Elena.

Squatting down beside her, he said, "We gotta do something."

Nodding, she let him help her up. They walked towards the door and would have made it, if all hell hadn't broken loose.

A blast hit the mountain, and the ground shook

beneath them. Several fell to the ground, tumbling over cushions, and Rhys and Elena steadied themselves against the door.

"They're hitting the lower wall!" Cara said.

Elena believed it. From the vibrations she reckoned they were doing a constant barrage, two volleys at a time, at least four lines. Depending on how many cannons they had in total and how much ammo, they could reduce the whole front face of the harbor wall within seven minutes.

Ripping the door open, Rhys stepped out onto the narrow walkway that led to a steep staircase. Of the four guards that were supposed to be posted outside, only one stood there now. He looked at them warily.

Rhys spoke to him quickly in Charneki, but he didn't look convinced. Rhys motioned at the others in the room, closed the door again, said more hurried words.

She didn't know what finally won him over, but without much more argument, she and Rhys were climbing the stairs, the guard hanging back to make sure no one else left.

Following Rhys across the courtyard at breakneck speed, they soon came to one of the top landings of the palace. The scene below them was chaos. Guns hammered the harbor wall, rocks and debris flying every which way. They had made mincemeat out of the gate, and already vehicles streamed into the lagoon-like harbor.

Charneki bodies were swarming, trying frantically to find shelter. It looked like warriors were ready to meet the incoming human attack, but civilian Charneki were close behind them, fleeing.

"Where's the queen?" Rhys asked.

Elena shook her head. "Shouldn't she be here?"

They looked down at the harbor. At each other. Then they careened down the staircase, making for Elena's cruiser, still parked just outside the gate.

Jumping into the driver's seat, she slammed the pockmarked door shut and smacked her hand against the start-up protocol. In the two seconds the cruiser took to come alive, she pulled her handgun from the compartment between her and Rhys's foot space.

"The rifle's under your seat," she told him, talking him through how to charge and reload it as she turned the cruiser downhill, the tires squealing.

Flying down the main street, Elena swerved this way and that, Charneki hurriedly diving out of their way. Rhys leaned out his window, calling out, Elena guessed, if anyone had seen the queen.

She had to grab Rhys's jacket to keep him inside as they went skidding across the street, no doubt leaving tire marks.

He slumped back into his seat, pale. "She went down to the harbor," he said breathlessly.

The cruiser hummed beneath them, and at the sight of the coming human army, Elena wished they had been able to steal an armed one. Their downward trajectory and the floored gas had them going faster than they should have been, and it was all Elena could do to keep them from ramming into Charneki.

Screaming past the second wall, it seemed most of the civilians were above the battle now, Elena and Rhys hitting the back lines of the Charneki army. She had to slow, use her horn, and Rhys leaned out the window again.

She swerved just in time to avoid a cannon blast which made a gaping hole in the road.

"Damn, they've broken through."

Rhys looked at her with a sort of sickened dread.

She slammed on the breaks, coming to a screeching stop when they saw a large mass of warriors moving up the slope slowly, the queen in the middle of the pack.

Opening his door, Rhys hung out, waving his hands and calling to them.

When the warriors saw them, they made towards them quickly, Yaro covering their dash.

The queen didn't hop in immediately, and Elena's thumbs beat against the steering wheel when she saw the first wave of vehicles switching to terrestrial mode and coming up onto the mountain.

The queen argued with Rhys and Yaro until Elena pressed her palm into the horn.

"You can't do anything if you're dead!" she said with fierce eyes.

Though she didn't have the translator on, the queen didn't seem to need it.

Yaro said something, and Rhys nodded. Finally the queen grudgingly pulled herself into the backseat.

Rhys and Yaro exchanged quick words before Elena backed up, turned around, and gunned it back up the mountain.

Splitting her attention between the road in front of her and the battle in her mirrors, Elena veered this way and that, noticing that those civilians not yet behind the second wall were injured or old.

The queen seemed to notice too and grasped both Elena and Rhys's shoulders.

"She wants to help them," he said.

Elena nodded but didn't stop. One thing at a time.

Once they were past the second wall, Elena stopped when the road forked around a large fountain.

Opening the translator on her gauntlet, she said, "You two go from here. I'll go back down for more."

Nodding, Rhys and the queen jumped out. The moment their doors shut she made a circle around the fountain and headed back outside the wall.

Stopping at the first group of injured Charneki she saw, she hopped out, the vehicle still running, and motioned for them to come with her. They were hesitant, even as the translator told them she would take them up.

They looked at her warily as she opened up the hatch door, revealing the compartment that usually carried a dozen human soldiers. There was room enough for about five crammed Charneki, and she could have at least one in the cab with her.

Shouts and struggling from further down the mountain seemed to convince them, and soon the ablest of the group were helping her load the others. When they were all in, Elena headed up, delivering them to the fountain.

As she passed through the second wall's gate for another batch, she saw the queen and Rhys standing atop the wall, the queen giving orders.

Elena made six runs in total before she started taking the worst of the wounded warriors up. She found Yaro in the fray, and through the translator told him what she wanted to do. Bearing three warriors with garish open wounds, she pushed the cruiser as hard as she could.

She made eight more runs, each one getting shorter as the Charneki line was pushed back.

"We must get back behind the market wall," said Yaro, "and hold them from there." A line of bluish blood already trickled from the left corner of his mouth.

"I can make one more run as you go."

With his nod of approval, Elena began backing up.

She felt it would happen before it did—a blast hit her front right tire, sending the cruiser onto its side with a deafening crash. Feeling like a rag-doll, Elena bounced about in the cab until the cruiser came to a rest, all of the glass smashed. Her ears rang as she blinked, trying to get her bearings.

Pulling herself up, she climbed out the sun roof, glass scraping against her forearm, tearing it. Her vision swam, but she willed herself to hold it together.

The cruiser was a heap of dented metal, and Elena wanted to mourn for it. The front passenger side had been almost completely blown off, and she thought how lucky it was they hadn't put anyone up with her for that run.

The noise of the battle slowly came back to her, and she looked over her left shoulder, still dazed, to see the coming human army, the cannons swinging this way and that, firing at anything that moved. The Charneki line was backing up steadily, making for the second wall, but more and more of them fell to gunshots.

She blinked rapidly. Ran to the back of the cruiser. Wrenched open the hatch. The warriors inside were alive, but worse for wear. Leaning down, she put her hands underneath the nearest one's arms and heaved.

For being lithe, the Charneki were heavy. As she strained, she called out, "Help me!"

She dragged her warrior over broken glass and bits of metal, continuing to yell for help, and she worried her words were lost in the fight.

Two warriors ran up to her then, started pulling the others from the cruiser, and she told them they had to get away from the vehicle, for it might explode. They made quicker work than her, and she tried keeping up when she saw how close they were to the front line.

The warrior to her left dropped, and Elena

almost jumped. She stared down at him. Shot in the head.

Her heart skipped a beat when she saw Oscar Livermore standing not far off in full combat gear, his rifle raised. He had been Sgt. White's other apprentice, Elena's sibling of sorts, and she hated him.

He turned his gun on the wounded warrior the other had been helping, and Elena dropped her warrior, going for her gun.

His barrel aimed at her next as her hands came up. She didn't have time to aim. Shot.

He lurched back, hit in the shoulder. When he straightened, he bared his teeth at her.

She put herself between him and the Charneki, told the latter to keep moving. She shot him again, in the chest, hitting his vest.

Recovering, he aimed at the Charneki again.

"Don't!" she warned, taking a step towards him. "You wouldn't. You'd be as bad as O'Callahan."

She levelled her gun at his head, knew she had

at least one shot left, not sure how many more. "Don't."

He took the shot. So did she.

He fell backwards, his eyes blank, and Elena heard another Charneki fall down behind her.

She stood there, in the middle of the street, shaking a little. There was no coming back from this. She had chosen her side.

Suddenly Yaro was in front of her. She didn't need the translation to know he was telling her to get moving.

Nodding numbly, she set herself to hauling her warrior again. Yaro picked up the other, and they left the rest; there was nothing to do for them now.

As she pulled the warrior up the street, the remaining warriors buying them as much time as they could, she couldn't avoid looking at Oscar's body, lying there in the street. She didn't know it would feel like this.

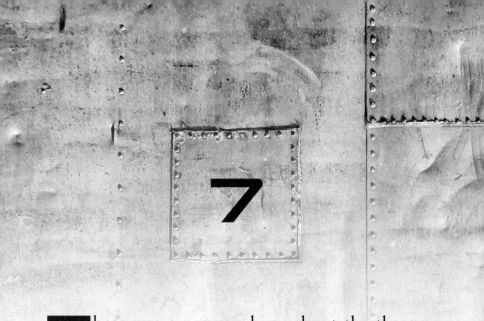

7

There was a nervous buzz about the throne room, and Rhys tried not to let his face betray how anxious he was too. The queen's council was sparser in number than usual and debated what to do now.

Hammond's forces had been stopped at the market wall, Karak surviving the night. But at first light, the bombardment started. Even now the mountain shook, their hearts beating in time to the echo of cannon blasts. The human offensive was divided into four groups, each attacking a different section of wall. Though the humans had forced their way onto the mountain, they suffered casualties and damage in the harbor, having to funnel in. Hammond wanted several points of entry this time around.

"How long d'you think they can hold out?" Cara whispered.

"Since the cannons are split up, maybe midday before a hole is made," said Elena.

The council seemed to have the same grim notion. The question wasn't if the humans would break through, but what needed to be done once they did.

The queen on her throne was a somber picture. Her iridescent skin was a grayish purple rather than its normal violet. She looked impossibly tired, sitting there with barely any queenly trappings. She rubbed her eyes.

Into the throne room came a warrior, running as fast as they could, screaming, "More have come! Golden One, they have come!" The noise was deafening, and Rhys winced as it echoed in the domed hall.

It was silent for a long moment before the queen asked, her voice barely above a whisper, "What did you say?"

"The reinforcements you sent for—they have come! Brave Ones from the eastern slopes and recruits from the midlands."

"How many?" she asked, sitting upright.

"A thousand from the east and six-hundred from the midlands."

Now the room buzzed with a sort of relieved excitement, but it was still subdued. Would those numbers be enough to retake the city?

"Have those from the southern hills come?"

"No, Golden One, we have not seen their standard."

She took a deep breath. "We must plan without them then. Do we know how large the human force is?"

Rhys nudged Elena and repeated the question. "*Mara*," he said, drawing her attention.

"The human troops number around five thousand, with as many as two hundred vehicles. Probably more," Elena said.

Once the translation was done, the queen looked

a little deflated. Rhys felt so too. Five thousand troops with large artillery, on top of the thousand Tikshi who survived the first battle now stood ready to take Karak.

"How many of ours can fight?" the queen asked.

"We have three thousand able-bodied warriors behind the market wall, with another three thousand wounded. Some might be able to fight—all would for the *mara*," Yaro said.

"From what we can guess, there are about four hundred outside the gate, under guard," said one of the captains. "There are probably some left in Oria as well, but we cannot be sure how many."

This didn't seem to hearten the queen. In the scheme of things, the Charneki still outnumbered the human force. Especially if civilians were willing to fight, they could overwhelm the humans ten to one. But civilians didn't always make good soldiers, Rhys knew. Usually they were fodder.

The decimation of the Charneki's forces was hard for Rhys to rationalize. He had seen for himself the full Charneki army on their march to San Angelo. More than twenty-thousand strong, the humans had chipped away at this force until it was reduced to three thousand able bodies. Rhys could barely wrap his head around the death toll.

The queen lifted her head after a long moment of consideration. "I have a plan for what we should do," she said, "and I ask you to listen to it, though you will not like it."

This caused a wave of uneasiness.

Leaning forward in her seat, she said, "I feel we must lose the battle to salvage the war."

The council stood stunned for a moment, until an Elder asked, "You would give up Karak? Your seat? Surely you cannot—"

"I would give up nothing, Wise One. I suggest leaving behind a small force—enough to convince the humans we are all putting up a fight. This force would stall them as I take the rest of the army north."

"To what end?" asked another Elder.

"They have dared to attack our home, and I

will do the same. Without their army, their city will be undefended. With its surrender, their army will have no choice but to give up Karak and either fight us in the north or sign a treaty."

Rhys saw this plan sat bitter in their mouths. Having the reinforcements charge the city probably sounded better to them, but it was the queen's decision to make.

Stepping forward, he said, "If we went north, we could meet those humans who resist our *mara*. They might open New Haven to us. If the Golden One makes an agreement with them and they convince others too, the human army would have no support at home."

"You have spoken with these others?" asked a captain.

He nodded. "Yes. Their leaders are willing to talk. The further north we go, the more I can speak with them."

"But what of everyone else?" asked another Elder.

"They must seek refuge in the mountain. Draw

everyone into the tunnels. I will take the army down the northeast passage and meet with the eastern forces. Chieftain Baravar, you and a small guard will take those who are able down the south passage and go inland. Those who cannot go will be hidden in the tunnels."

"Who will stay behind with the smaller force?" asked a captain.

"This is not an easy thing I ask. I would have someone do this for me—I do not wish to force anyone."

Stepping off of the dais and kneeling before the queen, Yaro said, "I will do this for you, *mara*. It would honor me to defend your city."

From the queen's expression Rhys knew she hadn't wanted Yaro to volunteer. No doubt she had hoped another of her captains would do the task. But there it was.

"It is you who honors me," she said, her eyes glassy. "Defend our home well, for I will miss you dearly on campaign."

Rhys's eyebrows shot up when Elena stepped forward. "I'll stay too," she said.

The queen nodded. "It would help greatly, I think, to have human knowledge on our side. Thank you, Brave One. You honor me as well."

Rhys touched Elena's shoulder. "You know this is a suicide mission—you should come north."

"Nah. I'm needed here. I might be able to do some good." One side of her mouth inched up. "Take care of yourself, okay?"

He swallowed the lump in his throat. "You too."

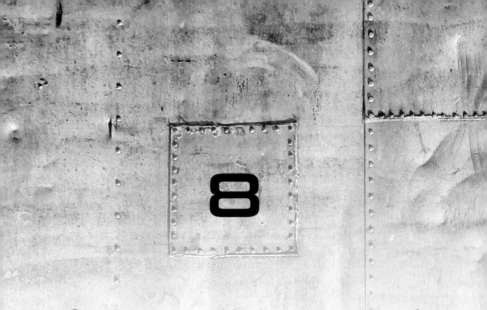

8

Alarms screamed in their ears, just enough warning to look up before the warehouse descended into chaos. Hugh looked towards the main door, which the watchdogs were trying to barricade. He could hear banging on the other side.

The team gathered together in small groups, looking at each other, deciding what they should do. They all knew who was on the other side. The question was, should they help to resist or take the risk and let the opposition in?

They all hit the ground when a shot went off in the warehouse. Someone cried out, asked what they thought they were doing. Did they want to set the weapon off right here?

When Hugh looked again, one of the doors was bent back, the barrel of a gun trying to find the watchdogs.

His insides felt knotted together, indecision eating at him. He could hear Rhys in his head, telling him that this was the moment, if there ever was one, to *do something*. The weapon had never sat well with him—handing it over to the opposition seemed the safest thing to do, to keep it out of Hammond's hands. Now was his chance.

His stomach grew cold from lying on the ground, his hands shielding his head as another shot ricocheted off the roof of the warehouse.

"Let them in, dammit!" one of the engineers yelled. "Before they hit it and we all die!"

Hugh suspected the opposition hadn't been aiming for the weapon, but threatening to did its job. When the soldiers remained deaf to the warning, some of the team got up, stalked up to them, and started wrestling their weapons away. More shots went off and two scientists stood, putting their bodies between the guns and the weapon.

With the soldiers occupied, the opposition had an easier time breaking down the barricade, and soon Ulysses Carter and others were climbing over. Hugh saw how they had so easily gotten into the facility: Cass walked behind Carter.

All the opposition members streaming into the warehouse were armed, not just with handguns, but with rifles and semi-automatics. So many projectiles in a room with a weapon of mass destruction didn't make Hugh feel any better.

The soldiers and engineering team were grouped up against one wall as Carter and some others looked over the weapon. He couldn't bring himself to look at Cass, though she was trying to catch his gaze. She looked so odd, holding a rifle. She didn't have a stomach for violence, but here she was, fighting her cause. And where was he? Against a wall, knowing he couldn't bear to tell her why it was he wouldn't fight.

Striding over to them, Carter looked at each person, though he paused a moment longer on Hugh. "Some weapon you've made here," he said. "Are you proud of yourselves? How could you do this?"

"It wasn't like we had a choice," said an engineer.

Carter frowned at him. "You always have a choice. And I want you to make one now." Hugh could feel Carter's eyes boring into him as he continued. "We brought our past with us to this new planet, and it's time we learn from our mistakes before we destroy this home too. As you know, General Hammond is pounding the native capital. What you don't know is that there's a native army headed right for us."

They gawked at him, wondering how he knew that. Hugh swallowed hard. Was it Rhys? Did that mean he was all right? Was he coming now, at the head of another army?

135

"Now, the general would be all too happy to see us fight them. But the general's not here. We intend to broker a truce with the natives. We have the support of the majority of civilians here, and President Kimura of San Angelo has confirmed that he'll back a treaty. The natives will walk through our perimeter and start negotiations in a few days. The future is here, so I'll ask you now, are you going to help us, or keep us in the past?"

When he met with further silence from his audience, Carter pressed on, "We need people who know the weapon here to guard it, in case the general gets any ideas. When she hears of what's happened, she'll no doubt return to New Haven. But united, we'll defeat her."

Unsurprisingly, the soldiers refused to do anything but stand there stonily, a hard glare on their faces, but several of the engineering team came forward, saying they wished to help.

Carter accepted all these new recruits graciously but looked at the rest with a sort of righteous disappointment. Turning this upon Hugh, Carter took a step forward. "He's coming, you know. With them."

"That sounds like him."

"You'd really undermine all he's trying to do?"

Finally Hugh met Carter's gaze and frowned. "I couldn't undermine him even if I tried."

———

Zeneba swayed with the steady lumber of the *garan* beneath her. The foothills flattened here, meadows of white and blue *julla* flowers following Nahara and Undin across the sky. The way the road cut through the meadow was lamentable.

By midday the Forest of Kara'olla would stretch out before them, and she didn't intend to stop the long column of warriors until they were deep into its heart. If she could, she would have them press on until they reached the north, but she knew her warriors had to be rested, able to fight. She would have to bear the next two days with patience.

Just over six thousand warriors marched behind her, and she could only pray to the Sunned Ones they would be enough. Over a thousand of these were already wounded; even greater was the number of civilians and volunteers. She would not trade them. To be a Brave One did not mean to wield a sword, but to have the courage to stand and shield all you held dear.

They had left through the mountain tunnels as planned, waiting just long enough to see Chieftain Baravar off with his column of civilians. Those who hadn't been able to flee took refuge in the cliff caves where they would be safe from discovery until Zeneba reclaimed Karak.

Her heart swelled to think on the bravery of her people. Not only had Yaro, much of her Guard, and a regiment of warriors stayed behind, but many civilians remained to support them and round out the ruse.

Blinking quickly, Zeneba looked about her, knowing what pain she caused herself by entertaining these thoughts. She grinned to see Rhys riding alongside her, a modified Charneki cuirass adorning his chest. She herself had drawn the sacred runes upon his cheeks, *mir* for courage and *unhuil* for valor.

"You are sure these rebels will speak with us?" she asked him.

"They want peace, *mara*. They will not want to fight you."

"Can they be trusted?" Ondra asked. She wished he had stayed with those wounded who were able to get into the caves, but she still drew strength from the sight of him in full armor, riding his *garan* as proud as any other Brave One.

Rhys nodded. "I know their leader. He will speak the truth with you, *mara*."

"But will this be true when your *mara* returns?" said Ondra.

Zeneba didn't feel heartened at Rhys's small hesitation.

"I believe yes. They do not trust her. They want a new *mara*."

She was slightly surprised when Ondra seemed content. She didn't know what caused it, but Ondra had, of late, given up his distrust of Rhys. It was a welcome change.

"And when we reach your city, they will be waiting for us?" she said.

Rhys nodded again. "They will open our wall to you. Their leader will speak for our other city too."

"What is this leader's name?"

"Ulysses Carter."

"That is an interesting name. Are all human names like this?"

"Ulysses was a legendary human. He fought a war for ten cycles and then rode the sea for another ten."

"Did your home have so much sea?"

Rhys grinned. "Yes. But it is a story about wandering. Humans wander much, I think."

It wasn't in Charneki nature to wander, to be

restless, but she supposed there was a sort of poetry about it. It certainly seemed the humans wandered among the stars to come to Charnek.

"What did he do after sailing the sea?"

"He finally returned home to his mate and son."

She smiled. "I like this story. You shall have to tell me more of your human stories when we're done."

He bowed his head. "It would honor me to tell them to you."

"Let us hope we return home much sooner than your wanderer."

Zeneba couldn't bear to be from Karak for ten cycles, for her heart was there, and she didn't think she could do without it for that long.

"Get back, get back!" Elena shouted, running as fast as she could backwards.

The palace gate gave way with a sickeningly

loud *bang*, and jade, iron, and red stone went flying in all directions. A piece of something glanced off her right arm, and she grimaced, feeling the skin tear.

A plume of dust shrouded the opening in the wall, the gnarled gate cast in shadow, like something from a nightmare. White hot gunshots came out of this cloud as if of their own doing, and Elena hit the ground, shielding her head with her hands.

She counted. When she heard a lull in the volley, she jumped up, found Yaro in the mayhem, and they bound up the palace steps with other Charneki. Bodies fell on all sides of her. Her hands worked furiously to reload her rifle, and Yaro covered her with his bow.

But it didn't stop the human army. They crashed over the palace, ready to consume it.

Elena secured the rifle against her shoulder, aimed. Took shoulder shots, legs. Tried not to make her shots fatal if she could help it. In all the dust and debris, that was difficult.

She ended up with a small band of warriors on one of the two semi-circular balconies on the tier just below the throne room. They used the rail somewhat for cover—it went up to Elena's chest—and as a vantage point to see the destruction all the way down to the crumbling harbor. The main promenade was lined with rubble and bodies, the road scorched with lines of black. They could just make out small pockets of movement; civilians and wounded warriors huddled together under armed guard.

Another group got onto the other balcony, across the stairs, and Elena realized with a throb to her neck that they were the last. A dozen now stood where the queen had left two-hundred.

Her gun clicked. Elena ripped at her gun belt and felt nothing. She looked down. Out. She swung the rifle over her back, knowing she could use it as a blunt object if need be.

There was a guttural cry to her left, and Elena looked just in time to see Yaro stagger back, a sizzling hole in his breastplate. She tried to catch him, and they fell together.

His face contorted in pain, the iridescent swirls of skin not settling on a color, shifting between red, blue, and black. The armor had stopped the worst of the shot—he didn't have a clean hole through him—but the skin beneath was gone, revealing purplish-gray muscle that oozed blue blood.

Tearing her jacket off, Elena pressed it to the wound, and told him over and over to keep pressure on it.

He waved her away. *"Zai-ohnn rua bua."*

She wouldn't leave him, and she took the moment to turn on her translator to tell him such. "You're not gonna die on me now. No way."

"You must save yourself," he said, wincing through the words. "Go to the other humans. Say you are our prisoner."

"No chance. I'm with you 'til the end."

His mouth a grim line, he nodded.

They realized at the same moment that it was

quiet. She looked up and saw soldiers standing along the steps, guns trained on them. The Charneki warriors were putting their weapons down.

The soldier with the gun pointed at Elena jerked the barrel. "Get up," he barked.

She nodded, putting her hands in the air, and slowly stood.

"It too."

Elena and Yaro glared at the soldier together, and the Charneki got up, though much more slowly. She moved half a step back so that he could lean on her, but he didn't, a defiant glint in his eyes. His skin rippled into a rich maroon.

She tried to swallow, but her mouth was too dry. She licked her lips, her tongue like sandpaper. What a way to end.

General Hammond didn't keep them waiting much longer. Two soldiers parted, allowing her to step onto the balcony and face the five Charneki and one turncoat.

Elena waited for some reaction from the general,

a gloat, a sneer, anything. But the general only looked the six of them over with mild disgust, and her hard expression was perhaps the most terrifying thing Elena had ever seen.

She thought she should be more frightened, but a sort of peace settled over her. There was no ambiguity, no escape. She knew the moment drew near. She only hoped they had bought Rhys and the queen enough time.

General Hammond nodded at the ground. "On your knees."

Stiffly, Elena complied. The Charneki followed her example, putting their hands behind their heads.

The general paced before them, her steps slow and deliberate, and stopped in front of Elena and Yaro. Elena knew he must stick out, his armor adorned with gold plates, different from the more uniformly armored warriors.

Yaro lifted his head to meet the general.

Her nostrils flared, and she lashed at his head,

the butt of her pistol connecting with his jaw. Elena winced.

Yaro's chest rose and fell quickly. He straightened, lifting his head again. Blood trickled from a corner of his mouth.

"Where's your queen?" Hammond asked, barely waiting for the translation before striking Yaro again.

He looked up at her, his mouth sealed shut.

"Where is she, dammit?"

When he still would not answer, the general went down the line of Charneki, pointed her gun at the warrior, and asked again. She did not need long to see they wouldn't answer. She fired, her gun echoing against the clear afternoon, and the warrior's body slumped backwards.

She went to the next one, but still neither Yaro nor the others would answer her. Another warrior *thumped* to the ground.

Seeing this wouldn't get her anywhere, she returned to Yaro and turned the gun on him.

"Tell me where she is and I'll think about sparing him," the general hissed at Elena.

"She's dead." Elena's voice sounded foreign to her ears, hoarse and deep.

The general snorted, turning away from Elena.

"Where. Is. Your goddamn. Queen?" said Hammond through gritted teeth.

Yaro's gaze travelled slowly up to meet hers. His lip twitched. The frown fell from his face, and he closed his eyes, his skin rippling into a deep purple.

She shot him.

Elena's stomach almost heaved, and her eyes stung. She bared her teeth at the general, her chest aching.

The general cocked her gun, centering it on Elena's head. "I haven't forgot about you, you worthless piece of sh—"

Loud static erupted from the general's comlink, and as Elena's pulse hammered in her head, the general turned away, adjusting the frequency with one finger.

"You're fading in and out, I can't—"

" . . . taken . . . opposition . . . going to let . . . coming north," got through.

"Repeat message. Over."

"Opposition has taken New . . . going to . . . natives."

The general's face fell, and Elena watched as a seething rage, cold and wrathful, settled over Hammond. She was nearly shaking.

Without looking back at Elena and the remaining warriors, the general began flying down the stairs, shouting orders as she went. They were leaving for New Haven.

Elena dared to take an uneasy breath. The soldiers looked around, slightly confused as to who should stay and who should follow the general. She took advantage and forced herself to look down at Yaro.

His colored skin had settled into black. His mouth was cracked open, his eyes closed. Blood pooled under his head.

She turned her head left when she heard a sound. The other two Charneki were looking at Yaro as well, their skin dark blue. A soft hum emanated from their throats, the tune low and sad. After a few more notes, Elena hummed too.

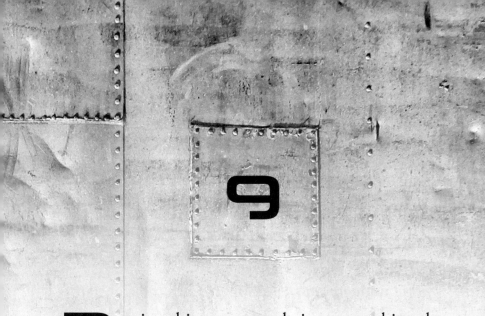

9

Despite this moment being everything he had worked for, Rhys's stomach was twisted into knots. Having left the main Charneki army half a mile outside New Haven, he, the queen, Ondra, and the Chieftains rode towards Carter and others of the opposition.

Carter smiled when he saw Rhys. "It's good to see you."

"You too. I'm glad my message got through."

Carter looked at the queen once they had dismounted. "This is her?"

Rhys nodded. He knew the queen had many official titles, but he felt it almost arrogant to think he could pronounce them all and in the right order. He contented himself by saying, "She is Zeneba Mara, their queen."

The queen nodded at Carter as Rhys said to her in Charneki, "This is him who I spoke of, *mara*."

She grinned. "The wanderer?"

"Yes. He would like to speak with you himself."

She nodded, and Rhys opened up the translator program on his gauntlet.

"I do not wish you or your people harm," the queen began, "but you must understand that as we speak, your *mara* is destroying our home. I do not want to have to do the same."

"I didn't like her decision to go to your city. I hope you know that not all humans are like her," said Carter.

They shared a look, and Rhys dared to hope this might go well.

Following Carter up the slight slope to the outskirts of New Haven, they found others of the resistance gathered there. Rhys was relieved to see

Jana, not too worse for wear. There was also a growing crowd hovering at the first line of buildings about two hundred yards away.

"You've got their support?" Rhys asked, nodding at the civilians.

"A majority," Carter said. "A lot of them are scared—Hammond's done a good job demonizing the Charneki. But they seem to understand the Charneki are a better option than the general. They don't want another fight like San Angelo."

"Will they stand up to the general, if it comes to that?" Rhys knew he had to prepare himself for the worst—General Hammond could be on her way here already.

Carter didn't look as confident as Rhys would have liked, but he said, "If it comes to it, yeah, I think so. They've seen we can stand up to her." He left Rhys then to join the others of the resistance while the Charneki formed a semi-circle, the queen at the center.

"I am heartened that I can speak reasonably to

one of you," the queen said. "I believe we might have peace here, if we are only wise enough to listen."

"We agree. Now, your majesty, I think you have terms?" said Carter.

The queen nodded. It had been decided upon that the resistance would act as a diplomatic body, in effect surrendering to the Charneki. This was to respect Charneki war code, which enabled the queen to make an executive decision on terms rather than weigh the opinion of all her Chieftains. Each side would offer terms of this "surrender," which would, ideally and in theory, start talks aimed at a treaty.

"First, the Charneki require sufficient technology to defend ourselves from any future human attack. What this may mean can be negotiated later, but a deterrent is necessary. We would also like to establish a flow of learning between our two people—there is much we might teach you humans about the land, for I understand you are here to stay."

"Yes, your majesty, we are."

She nodded. "Then we Charneki must accept that. But there is the issue that these were our lands. You have taken away homes, and I want them restored to those who choose to reclaim them. The *buna* mines will be reopened, and we will dig there jointly. You will also be allowed further south for farming purposes, though exact locations must be discussed, in exchange for an open trade between our people. Once your crop has been established, twenty percent will go to Karak in war reparations, to feed our displaced and wounded, for the span of five cycles. After that we may renegotiate. These are the Charneki terms for your city's safety. Have you anything to say?"

Carter took a moment to confer quietly with the others. It couldn't all be sitting well, especially not the twenty percent reparations, but their dislike didn't change the fact that there was a native army not half a mile away.

"We accept these terms and only ask that our

current farmland be respected and that we be allowed to establish other human settlements."

Now it was the queen's turn to look displeased, but an agreement was Karak's only salvation.

"These are acceptable terms. I am pleased you speak with—"

Jana suddenly gripped Carter's arm like a vice, holding her gauntlet in front of him so that he could see the message.

"Goddamn," Rhys heard Carter mutter. "That was too quick."

Rhys only had to see the others of the resistance start moving back to New Haven, shouldering their guns, to know what was happening. They needed to mobilize. Now.

"Rhys, she's coming!" Carter said. "Get them behind the perimeter and we'll reactivate it. That might slow her down!"

The queen didn't even need the translation, sending two Chieftains off to rally the army and bring them into the borders of the perimeter while three others waved great colored banners, their embroidered threads sparkling in the sun. The army became a great sea of movement.

Rhys looked up at the queen, his heart in his throat. "I did not think she would come so soon," he said.

The queen shook her head. "Do not be troubled, little one. Our plan has worked—if she is here then she is not in my city, and for that I am thankful."

Rhys nodded, trying to feel heartened. It didn't quite work.

Hugh looked up when he felt something moving the air in front of him. Cass was squatting down in front of him. His head slumped back down into the dark crevice of his folded arms. He hadn't heard her replace his guard.

Though he had been allowed to return home, the resistance felt he knew too much about the weapon to be left alone. He had spent the past days under house arrest, an armed resistance fighter outside his door at all times.

He could barely see her in the glum light of the apartment, but he knew it was Cass. None of the other guards would come in.

When she still didn't say anything, Hugh raised his head again.

She swallowed, just staring at him for a long moment. "How're you doing?"

He shrugged.

Sitting down, she folded her arms on her bent knees, mirroring his own position against the wall. "I didn't want them to keep you prisoner."

He shrugged again. "It could be worse."

"Yeah, I guess."

He stared at her. "Did you want something, Cass?"

"I wanted to see how you were."

"I'm fine." He rested his head back on his arm. "Hugh, look at me."

He wouldn't.

She kicked the toe of his boot with her own. "Look at me." Finally, when he had lifted his head just enough so that one eye could see her, she said, "I don't want you to be mad at me."

"I'm not."

"Really? Because you're being pretty passive aggressive right now."

"No, I'm not."

They fell into silence again, and Hugh hated himself. The only things he had ever kept from Cass was what his job required him to hide. Now he hid behind a wall of apathy rather than admit the truth to her. Or himself.

"Hugh," she touched his elbow, "I want you to join the resistance."

He scoffed. "Why? What difference would it make?"

She frowned. "A lot. We need everyone."

He shook his head. "Nothing I do is gonna make a damn bit of difference."

"How can you say that?"

"What? It's the truth. What have I ever done that's made a difference?"

"How can you not care? Our future is at stake here—don't you wanna end this war?"

"That's what all rebels say. Besides, there's always gonna be another war."

"Are you trying to be aggravating? Because it's working."

"I'm trying to make you understand."

She scooted closer. "Please do. I want to understand, because nothing coming out of your mouth is making sense. I reserve the right to smack you, though."

Now that she had called him out and was sitting there expectantly, Hugh's tongue went dry. He hadn't meant to get backed into a corner, but that's exactly what she had done to him. He wanted to get rid of her, knowing the longer he talked the more he would reveal. And he feared what he would say.

After his mouth hung open for a moment, he said, "I'm tired."

"We're all tired of this war. That's why—"

"No, Cass, listen to me. I'm tired of trying. Everything I've done has been pointless. It didn't help anyone. If I'd kept my head down, it all would've happened the same. I don't make a difference, and I don't want to."

She gazed at him steadily through this speech and for some time afterward. "This is about Rhys, isn't it?"

Of course it was about Rhys. Everything was about Rhys. Hugh's entire life had been about Rhys, and as he sat there in the semi-darkness of his apartment, Cass looking him with equal measures of pity and disgust, he realized how much he resented that fact. His life had never been his own—whether it was thinking about Rhys, waiting for him, trying to help him, his life revolved around his brother. He didn't know what it was to be his own person.

He hid his face in his hands.

"Hugh, I'm not asking you to do this for Rhys. I'm asking you to do this for you. This is your home too. You can't sit there and tell me you're happy with how things are. This is your chance to change it."

"What if what I want to do is nothing?"

She took a breath. "I'm not going to force you to do anything, Hugh. That's the point—you should be free to do what you want. I wouldn't be badgering you, though, if I believed any of this 'wanting to do nothing' crap."

His eyes flicked to hers.

"I don't know what's going on with you," she said, "but whatever it is, it's got you scared. If you're not going to do anything, fine. But that should be your decision alone."

Hugh's chest hurt, and he couldn't look at Cass. She was right. He knew it, and so did she. But that didn't change the truth of how tired Hugh was. It didn't change that doing nothing was the first decision Hugh had made on his own in a long time.

Cass seemed to see she wasn't going to get any further with him, for she slowly unfolded her body, stretching out her back.

"I hope you come around, but whatever happens, we'll always be friends. Okay?"

He nodded.

She smiled down at him, and his icy resolve almost melted.

Cass opened her mouth to say something, but nothing came out, instead a static voice filling his cold apartment. Holding her gauntlet up to her ear, Cass's face was a mixture of shock and a frown.

Hugh could just hear the voice over the comlink. She was coming.

"Stay here," she told him. "Lock the door—don't come out 'til it's over!"

She flew from the apartment. The door slowly slid closed behind her.

Hugh sat there in darkness again, his eyes

burning a little from the imprint of light. He put his head between his knees, his fingers weaving into his hair. What now?

He took a ragged breath. The only thing his doing something had accomplished was getting Saranov killed. Saranov. The man who had stood by him when Rhys hadn't. How had Hugh thanked him?

Was he living in fear? Hell yes, he was. He was scared of everything going on outside his door.

He raised his head. Wiped at his eyes. Slowly got to his feet. Walked across the room to the door. Opened it.

Yeah, he was scared as hell.

10

Elena sat in the courtyard just above the former human captives' storeroom, grouped with forty or so Charneki. Most were those civilians who had stayed behind to help support the warriors.

The human unit still seemed baffled about there being so few, and Elena took it as a good sign. They hopefully wouldn't find the tunnels before the queen returned.

Now that was the question. She swallowed hard, trying not to linger on her pessimism. The queen would come back for her city. They bought her enough time.

Watching the two guards posted at the entrance of the courtyard through her lashes, Elena finished canvassing the perimeter. It wasn't the best plan she had ever had, but it would have to do.

Glancing at the Charneki next to her, called Ankha, Elena jerked her head towards the entrance.

"*Boneer ila vren sua, unhar-loa?*"

"Trust me," she said, though her translator was off and she could only guess what Ankha had actually said. She caught *unhar-loa*, 'little warrior.' That was Yaro's nickname for her. Yaro. She swallowed again.

Elena thought Ankha looked dubious, but she needed her to play her part. It had taken the better part of a day to convey her plan without a translator, and opportunities to do so had been few and far between. This had to work.

Slowly lying down on her side, Ankha tried her best to look in pain.

"Hey!" Elena shouted, jumping up, despite her

cuffed hands. The two guards looked over at her. "She needs help!"

One pointed his gun at her. "Get down!"

"Look, I think this's serious! Can't you get a doctor or something?"

"What the hell would a doctor be able to do for them?"

Elena made a face. "I mean one of their doctors."

"Half the city is worse off than her. She'll just have to tough it out."

She had to try hard not to let her eyes wander to the four warriors sneaking around behind the guards, hiding behind columns of the colonnade. "She might die. She's in a lot of pain."

"That's not our fault."

Her eyes widened when they began turning away from her. Licking her lips, she advanced another few steps, saying, "Yes, it is."

"What'd you say?"

"You heard me. You did this. The least you could do is not be cruel about it."

The guards had mirrored expressions of disgust and realization. The warriors didn't give them time to say anything else, setting upon them with great cries. Overpowering them, the warriors used a rock to break Elena's cuffs.

She grinned up at a warrior, one of the two who survived Hammond. "That wasn't so hard."

"*Mananahn, unhar-loa!*"

Turning her translator back on, she said, "I'm right behind you."

He bowed his head to her and then looked over her head to the others in the courtyard. "More will come," he said. "We must act now—we must retake the city!"

The others jumped to their feet, and all the weapons that could be found were taken up. For herself, Elena grabbed up all the arms she could carry from the two unconscious guards.

Running up along the colonnade, they came into a wide semi-circular garden. Jogging through this, they finally found the main staircase.

She looked up at the sound of shots and turned her gun towards the throne room. Five more soldiers came flying at them, but she got two before the warriors, brandishing their swords, set upon them.

"You," she said, pointing at a warrior, "look through the palace and see if there're others. And you, head into the city. Get everyone who's able!"

Hammond would be crazy to leave fewer than two-hundred soldiers with at least a unit of armored cruisers, New Haven besieged or no. If that were the case, and that was the best case, the forty of them with her rifle and two handguns would be about as much of a match for them as they were the first time.

"Take the palace!" her survivor warrior shouted. "We will have the high ground!"

Several others went running off to check other locales, but everyone else stormed up the stairs, meeting the dozen soldiers at the top. Warriors fell under fire, but it seemed their breastplates could take a hit and the shot wouldn't be fatal. But only one.

The wind was knocked from Elena, a punch to her gut, and she stumbled. She felt a hand on her shoulder, but she waved it off, pushed forward. She had to get to the top, had to cover them when more came.

Finally at the landing, the soldiers either dispatched or incapacitated, Elena ordered the Charneki take up all the guns they could find. Standing in front of them, she explained quickly how the guns worked, that they just had to aim and pull the trigger.

"*Unhar-loa*," said her warrior.

She looked over her shoulder. Here they were.

"Just aim and fire," she said. "Ready?"

The warriors shouldered their guns quickly, the civilians more hesitant.

"Fire!"

The humans weren't prepared for Charneki using guns, and though the natives' aim wasn't ideal, their volley kept the human unit from advancing further than the palace gate.

She called for them to stop when most of the unit had fallen back behind the wall.

Blinking through her swimming vision, Elena traded her handgun for the rifle, liking the solid feel of it against her shoulder.

A human peeked past the wall and met with a shot. It glanced off the palace wall but nonetheless drove them back.

The two suns beat down on them, and Elena worried that she might lose consciousness. She needed to keep it together—she had to see this through. She had promised.

As the moments trickled by, she worried this might turn into a stalemate. She didn't know how long she would last in a stalemate. Never patient, her throbbing abdomen urged her on.

An explosion of noise startled her back into cognizance. She could see a swarm of movement outside the palace, and Elena's heart beat quickly when she realized hundreds of Charneki were converging on the palace gate.

"We have them on both sides!" her warrior said, his skin flashing maroon.

The celebration was short lived, for the humans now took cover on their side of the palace wall, firing upon those in front of the throne room to cover their entry.

Ducking down behind the railing for cover, Elena decided that if she was going to go out, best it was in a firefight. Leaning her gun over the edge of the rail, she did what she did best, and shot.

The air sizzled with the spicy smoke of gunfire, and the red stone beneath them felt hot to the touch. They pounded the human line hard, but not as hard as the soldiers pounded the Charneki without guns outside the palace gate.

"*Unhar-loa,* we must do something!" said her warrior.

Nodding, she said, "Follow me."

Pulling herself up, she ignored the look the warrior gave her.

"Please, *unhar-loa,* you are—"

"I said follow me!" And she pounded down the staircase, giving him and the others no chance to stop her.

From their cries, she knew they followed. Their gunshots crackled, hitting the human line as they descended. The human line collapsed in on itself, taken by surprise, overwhelmed by the sea of bodies coming at them. And just like that, it was over.

Kicking a gun away from a soldier, she held her hand out, stopping the warriors.

The warrior and she stared the other down, but finally he nodded. "Disarm them. And sound our horn!" he cried out.

Several Charneki broke away from the group, heading deeper into the palace.

The warrior reached out and caught Elena when she stumbled. She tried pushing him away, told him not to worry, but found she couldn't stand anymore without his help.

Ankha came up beside her. "You are hurt! Please, *unhar-loa*, you must let us help you."

Elena touched a hesitant hand to her stomach, felt how drenched her tattered shirt was. "Damn," she muttered.

Ankha wrapped her arms around Elena. "Be easy. I have you."

Somehow Elena felt comforted to be in this Charneki's arms. Her ears filled with the hearty sound of the mountain horn, bellowing from the north face. She lifted her head with Ankha skyward, and they waited. One, two, three horns replied.

Ankha smiled down at her, flushing gold. "There are others. The city will be ours again!"

Elena smiled too. "Glad to help."

"Oh, *unhar-loa*, I will sing your praises until the day I die."

Elena nodded but honestly didn't hear much of what Ankha said. Her vision was gone, and her fingers were cold. Ankha cried out as she completely lost her ability to stand.

She could feel her flesh pulsing in her hand, warm and hot and red. Well then. Nothing for it now.

The perimeter didn't hold the general long, and soon a whole section crippled under cannon fire. The electricity sizzled out of the crumpled perimeter section, Hammond's forces rolling right over it and barreling towards the front lines of Charneki and resistance.

"Stay close to me," the queen told Rhys. "Ondra and I will protect you."

Shouldering the rifle he got from Carter, Rhys said, "You stay close to me this time."

She grinned down at him, and together they met the first wave of soldiers.

They came as a thunderous force, raining

gunshots, but unlike at Karak, this time it was answered by a counterattack of resistance guns combined with Charneki arrows.

Rhys realized he had tears in his eyes as he shot at the coming force. He wasn't really aiming, just holding his finger on the trigger, but he knew in his gut he couldn't have missed that often. His throat worked around trying to swallow, and he had to keep telling himself there would be a moment to feel guilty. Now he needed to fight.

The speed with which Hammond's army hit them almost broke their line, Charneki and resistance members flinging themselves out of the way of cruisers and speeders. For a moment everything descended into chaos, the line broken into pockets, until he heard the queen's horn.

He found the queen and Ondra, who was blowing the horn, and made his way, with several other Charneki, to them.

Some semblance of a line was reformed, and from what he could see of Carter and the others, he had managed to do the same for the resistance. They enveloped the soldiers who had gotten through and repelled a second wave.

For a few minutes it looked like they would be able to hold their ground, but then a convoy of cruisers with mounted cannons lumbered up to the front line, unleashing a barrage of cannon fire.

When the dust settled, Rhys saw that the line couldn't be reformed this time. The battle fragmented into small skirmishes between pockets of Charneki, resistance, and soldiers. Rhys was thankful that they got all the resistance to discard anything that looked like the military uniform, so that the Charneki could tell them apart.

The queen's group remained salient until finally pushed back. Taking cover behind a building, Rhys took the moment to reload as some of the warriors notched arrows to cover their retreat further into New Haven.

"She destroys her own city!" the queen said.

"It looks so."

She glanced down at him. "She would be queen of bodies and rubble?"

"If she is queen, then yes."

She just shook her head.

At a cry from one of the warriors, they doubled around to the south side of the building, and Rhys cringed to see they were headed straight for the residential quadrant.

"We cannot go further this way!"

"We do not have a choice," Ondra growled, setting upon a nearby soldier.

Hearing something rumbling to his left, Rhys turned in time to see a cruiser rolling towards them. Shouting out, his alarm bought them just enough time to avoid the first volley.

Bounding out of the way behind another building, Rhys hauled himself up to see the queen and the others across the street. His eyes went wide as the cruiser advanced, cannon swiveling around to take aim at the Charneki.

"No!"

Aiming his rifle, he let loose a series of shots at the windshield and passenger side window, pounding the cruiser with dents. His body vibrating, he had to stop a moment, sucked in a breath, and fired again. The queen and her warriors hurled spears into the cruiser.

When Rhys paused to reload, the passenger door opened and General Hammond herself stepped out. Rhys couldn't work his fingers fast enough; she held up a handgun and shot him.

He grunted, the wind knocked out of him, and he fell back against the building. He felt numb, his fingers trembling, and the new cavity in his chest quivered at the light of day.

Glancing to his left, he met General Hammond's disgustingly pleased look. Another cruiser sped up and she jumped in, barking an order to head to industrial. They had to get to . . . get to what? He had almost heard.

As hers and other cruisers sped past, Rhys

touched a shaking hand to his right shoulder. Putting pressure on it, he grimaced.

The queen suddenly squatted down in front of him, putting her hands on either side of his face. "Oh, Rhys, keep your eyes open! Look at me!"

He blinked furiously.

"Is it very bad?" she asked, looking at the wound. "I-I do not know your human bodies."

"Yes, I think it is bad."

Shaking her head, the queen ripped the sleeve off of her robe and balled it up, placing it against the wound.

"You need to get back to them," he said. "They need you."

"We will not leave you, Rhys."

He almost wept to hear her say that, for he didn't want to be left alone. He was scared out of his mind.

"Can we do anything for you, little demon?" asked Ondra.

"I think I need a healer."

With a wave of the queen's hand, a warrior ran from their group, off in search of a resistance member.

Gripping the material of Rhys's jacket, the queen gazed steadily down at him and said, "We will protect you, Rhys, but you must fight it."

Nodding, he said, "I will not go anywhere."

"Good."

"*Rhys!*"

The queen whirled around at the sound of an approaching human, and she crouched protectively over him, her bladed bow staff held behind her, ready to strike, as Ondra and the others jumped between her and the human.

"Which side does it fight for?" the queen demanded.

"That's my brother—please! Rhys, it's me!"

"*Mara*, it is my brother, please do not hurt him."

She nodded and told her warriors to stand down, though she herself took longer to move out of Hugh's way. The two of them stood there, staring at the other, and Rhys knew her thoughts were on the last time she and Hugh spoke. Finally, she let him pass.

Slumping to his knees beside him, Hugh put a shaky hand on Rhys's shoulder. "I-I saw her . . . "

Rhys shook his head. "It's nothing. I'll be fine."

Pulling the wad of cloth up a little, Hugh took a look at the wound and sucked air through his teeth. "My god, Rhys . . . "

Tears welled in Rhys's eyes. "Hugh, I-I don't wanna die."

Hugh shook his head and wrapped an arm around Rhys. It felt good to lean against him. He could feel Hugh's heart thumping in his chest.

"You're not gonna die on me. No way in hell."

Rhys winced. "It hurts now."

Hugh pressed his forehead against Rhys's. "You fight it, d'you hear me? You've done too much to quit now. You've made this world—don't leave it. Not yet."

He buried his face into Hugh's shoulder.

"I'm sorry."

"What?"

"I'm sorry," Hugh said, wiping at his eyes. "I-I've made a mess of things."

Rhys shook his head. "You did what you thought was right. I didn't make it easy."

Hugh sighed. "I need to do what's right now."

He frowned. "What?" Panic rose in his throat as Hugh steadied him against the building and made to stand up. Grabbing at him, Rhys said, "No, Hugh, wait, don't leave me, please!"

Balancing on the balls of his feet, Hugh said, "She'll be going for the bomb. I gotta stop her."

Rhys sat stunned at the word "bomb." He had heard rumors . . .

Hugh gripped Rhys's hand. "You stay strong, okay? I'll come right back. But I gotta do this, for you."

Swallowing the lump in his throat, Rhys finally nodded. "Come back quick."

After standing, Hugh looked up at the queen and said, "Will you watch him for me?"

She glanced down at Rhys, and though she didn't have a translation, she said, "Nothing shall happen to him."

Rhys watched Hugh's back as he ran after the line of cruisers towards the industrial quadrant. His felt sick, but not from the pain.

———————

A surge of warriors came charging out between buildings, rallying to Zeneba and her group, still protectively surrounding Rhys.

As they reformed a line across the convergence of two dirt streets, warriors reported that many had been backed out of the city with much of the human resistance. The human army was reclaiming the city, but their queen was nowhere to be found.

"We must capitalize on her absence," Zeneba said.

A great crashing sound ushered in a unit of human soldiers, and her warriors bared their swords and spears, metal glinting in the murky sunlight, Nahara trying to glimpse through the heavy dust.

"Let us see them now fight for their home," she said as loud as she could. "Let us make them regret ever setting eyes on the Red City!"

A great cry went up, and in a few stolen moments, Zeneba left a group of warriors in charge of defending Rhys. Their eyes locked, and she gave him a nod. "Until we see each other again, little one. In this life or the next."

"Nahara bless you, *mara*," he said.

"And Undin keep you, until I might."

She turned from him to face the advancing humans, knowing that should they break through, Rhys couldn't fight them off.

Raising one bladed end of her staff, she pointed it at the center vehicle and cried, "The ancestors see us now. Shall we meet them?"

"Tomorrow!" the warriors cried, and a smile flashed across her face.

As one, their skin rippled into a fiery red. She glanced to her right and caught Ondra's eye. He grinned.

They charged, no matter how the humans' weapons punched holes, broke them, made them bleed. The warrior to her left fell; she went on. They were so close—she could see the human inside the center vehicle.

She looked, startled, to her right, at the sound of a collective cry, and from the human flank came crashing Chieftain Heta and her remaining contingent. Her black armor gleaming, Chieftain Heta punished the soldiers, her warriors breaking the windows of the vehicles and tearing the humans from them.

Zeneba's warriors pounded them from the front, and the humans folded in on themselves, the vehicles crashing into each other in their haste to flee. They pushed, slashed, stabbed at them, forcing them back.

She clasped arms with Chieftain Heta as their forces met, and together they charged back out into the southern plain.

"The day isn't lost, Golden One," she said. "Most of the army is intact—they need only see sight of you."

"Then by all means, Brave One, let us meet them."

Her heart pumping and her lungs filled with renewed vigor, Zeneba caught sight of the army and the human resistance filling up the holes in their lines. Beside her, Ondra blew her horn and the army turned to see her making her way towards them. The nearest captain answered her call with his own, and at the second horn, the army marched to meet them.

"Zeneba!"

An all too familiar sizzle scorched the skin of her shoulder, and she winced, blood already oozing from a new wound. She stumbled, and her warriors tried to form a circle around her, but they couldn't defend her or themselves from the humans speeding towards them.

The vehicles skidded around them, kicking up dust, and she coughed, her wound stinging. Leaning on her staff, she readied herself in time to see a hulking human descend from the nearest cruiser. There was no mistaking the yellow head of her interrogator, and her upper lip twitched to see him.

His weapon levelled at her chest as he approached, but quickly swung right, aimed at Chieftain Heta, who sprung at him. Two *bangs* hit her black breastplate, and she fell in a cloud of dust.

Zeneba didn't let him point it at her again, whipped her staff through the air, brought it down in an arch, and split his weapon in two.

He sneered at her and met her as she rushed him. Getting a grip on her staff, he nearly wrenched it away, all his little teeth bared at her.

She bared hers at him, her nostrils flaring.

Pulling the staff back, she rammed her head against his, her helmet making a sickening sort of *thwack* against his skull. He reeled back, a cut above his left brow bleeding.

She realized too late that he was feigning, and he shoved her back against his vehicle. Her shoulder wound screamed in pain, and for a moment she thought she might lose consciousness. She pushed him back, regained her staff, and swung it up and down. Warm blood gushed onto her feet as he fell to his knees, a look of disbelief widening his eyes. She left him there, in the dust.

When she found Ondra again, she leaned against him. Her contingent and her interrogator's unit had nearly decimated each other.

She nodded at the army. "Take me to them."

"You need a healer."

"There will be time later." She gazed up at him. "We must finish this."

"Oh no."

Slumping to the ground, Hugh reached down and pulled a bloody Cass to him with shaking hands. She lay there shivering, clutching her lower abdomen.

"W-we couldn't h-hold them," she forced out. "T-too many."

"I-it's gonna be fine," he said. "You're gonna be fine."

She shook her head. "Have I ever told you you're the *worst* liar?"

"Don't say that," he said. "Don't you dare." Glancing over her head at the warehouse, the door wide open, he pulled off his jacket and pressed it against her midsection. "Cass, I need you to get outta here."

She frowned up at him. "Where're you going?"

"Someone's gotta stop her—I think I gotta try."

He stared at her, suddenly desperate for her to say something. He needed to know that despite what he wanted to do being terribly and utterly stupid, it was still what needed to be done.

"Help me up."

She winced the whole way, but, after taking a moment to steady herself, she was able to bear her own weight. Biting her lip, she looked over at him, her free fist full of his shirt.

"You get the hell outta there when it's done. If you don't, I'll be mad."

"I know better than to make you mad."

"Good," she said with a stiff nod, her eyes welling.

He knew if he didn't go then, he never would, so he turned from her, pausing only long enough to grab up a handgun and stash it between his belt and back.

"Hugh!"

He wouldn't look, couldn't.

Walking into the warehouse, he went straight for the big space in the back where the bomb was. He thought it was too easy to make it so far into the building, and came upon the general and her personal guard without being noticed.

"Then find someone to work it!" the general was saying, waving a gun about. Her soldiers watched it warily.

"But we can't use it on our own people!" an officer argued with her.

"Those traitors aren't our people. We're doing this for *our people*!"

"It was built to take down a mountain—what d'you think it'll do to New Haven?"

"We can't risk it!"

Hammond pointed her gun wildly between the officers, whose argument suddenly and unceremoniously died in their throats. Hugh thought she looked like a mess, strands of hair falling out of that once crisp knot at the base of her neck.

Her sharp eyes caught sight of him. "O'Callahan. Get over here!"

The others turned to see him, and two soldiers came over and hauled him in front of her.

Pointing with her gun behind her at the bomb, she said, "Get this thing operational."

His breathing erratic, he nodded. As he walked past, she pulled the gun out from his belt. This didn't ease Hugh's already hammering heart, for he knew more than just the general's hair was coming undone.

Hugh entered the startup prompt, bringing the command monitor to life. It took him only a moment to find what he was looking for. He almost smiled to see that he was right—Cass had been sabotaging it the whole time. It couldn't take out a mountain, not even close, but it could still do damage. If the resistance had tried to completely dismantle it, they hadn't had enough time.

He worked quickly, sweat tricking down the back of his neck as he felt the general watching him. The others shifted nervously, muddled voices plagued by static echoing from all comlinks. The native army had rallied, taken the residential quadrant, and was coming for the industrial. They needed the general.

Pressing her gun between his shoulder blades,

Hammond said, "Set it for ten minutes; that should be enough—"

"I can't."

She rounded on him, her eyes wide and wild. "What'd you say?"

"I can't. I've already set it for thirty seconds."

Most of the soldiers ran then, the fine tendrils of their loyalty finally snapping. The rest took slow steps back, cursed him, implored the general to come quick.

His eyes followed her gun as she continued to point it right at him. Tears and sweat pooled under her quivering lower lip.

"How could you? How could you betray your own kind?" she cried.

"My brother is my kind."

"*General!*" an aide screamed.

She squared her jaw.

"You shoot me, you hit this thing, and it goes off now, not in—" he looked, "—thirteen seconds."

She looked from him, to the weapon, to her

gun. Her mouth letting out a cry and a laugh at the same time, she turned the gun on herself.

Hugh balked as she fell to the ground, and her other soldiers ran for it. He glanced back at the time. Seven seconds.

Running in the opposite direction of the front door, he threw himself into the small room at the back of the warehouse, a sort of bunker designed as a contingency for failure during construction.

He just got the door shut and himself under the desk when flames engulfed the room, a deafening howl burned his ears, and the building tore itself apart.

Rhys cracked an eye open, watching the doctor's back as she left the room. He counted to five before easing up, careful not to irritate his shoulder. The wound prickled as he touched bare toes onto the cool metal floor.

Creeping over to the doorway, he checked to make sure none of his three roommates watched as he slipped into the corridor. The footsteps of a few people walking down the hall made small echoes, and Rhys pattered in the other direction. His heart pumped, dodging past open doors.

Making it down the hall, he stalked into the intensive care wing of the medical ward. Ducking into a room, he waited for two nurses to walk past before heading further into the ICU. His break-out, and planned break-in, wouldn't be possible if many patients hadn't been relocated to San Angelo just that afternoon.

He strained to remember the exact number of the room he wanted, almost skidded past the one with *O'Callahan, Hugh* on a projection next to door 16. His heart faltered as he walked into the room.

Hugh lay on the further of two beds in the room, the other lying empty. Rhys walked to him slowly, relieved to see the small rise and fall of his chest. He knew the doctors thought Hugh's chances were bleak—no one else within a two hundred yard radius of the detonation had made it out alive. His body was completely broken, his legs badly burned. He might never walk again, if he lasted that long. Rhys refused to believe it.

"I see we had the same idea."

Rhys nearly jumped out of his skin and whirled around to find Elena looking down at him.

"When did you get back?"

"Earlier today. And it's nice to see you too."

He nodded at the wad of bandages wound round her midsection. "You too?"

"Mm. Yours bad?"

"I've had worse."

Even in the haziness of early morning light, Rhys could tell she doubted that.

Picking at a hangnail on his thumb, Rhys said, looking at the ground, "I never thanked you."

"For what?"

"For defending Karak. What you did . . . it was really brave."

She nodded. "I hear you did pretty well yourself, little warlord."

Rhys grinned.

"D'you have any idea how ungodly early it is?"

They turned to see Hugh looking at them with barely-open eyes. One side of his mouth inched up as they came to stand beside his bed.

"Hey, idiot," Elena said.

Hugh winced. "I deserve that. I should've done what you said—I should've come with you." He laced his fingers with hers, and to Rhys's surprise, she didn't pull away.

She shook her head, her face sharp but her eyes glassy. "It doesn't matter now."

Hugh bit his lip, his eyes travelling down to their hands. "Elena, d'you . . . d'you think, if things had gone better, we . . . ?"

She pawed at her eyes. "Yeah."

He smiled, and she nodded.

"How's Cass?" he asked.

At that Elena pulled her hand away, hid her face. "She's mad at you. And I am too! You idiot!"

She retreated to the foot of his bed, her back turned to them, and Rhys replaced her at Hugh's shoulder.

"She's just worried," Rhys said, big tears running down his face as he spoke. "S-she thinks you're not gonna make it, but I-I know that you're gonna be fine."

Hugh smiled at him, and Rhys could feel his chest splitting apart.

"I'll do whatever you say," Rhys said suddenly with a hiccup, "you can boss me around all you want—but you have to stay."

Hugh managed a nod, though his eyes were barely little slits. He filled his fist with Rhys's shirt. "You'll do what Elena tells you, no matter what, okay?"

"Hugh, you—"

"Rhys."

"Yeah, yeah I will." His head slumped down onto the bed, pressed against Hugh's shoulder.

"Good. A-and . . . I want you to make your new world." He closed his eyes and grinned. "I can see it now. You just have to make it. I know you can."

Rhys shook his head. "Don't you dare leave me! I won't forgive you."

"I'm sorry I made you hate me, Rhys. I wish I could go back, do things right."

"I don't, Hugh, I don't hate you! I love you! It's

200

my fault—I should've done things right. It should be me, not you—I should've—"

"Stop it. I did this for you. Don't you ever forget that, okay?"

Somehow that hurt Rhys almost as much as the slow realization that Hugh's body wasn't going to heal.

"What's going on in here?" A doctor put his hand on Rhys's shoulder. "You shouldn't be in here—you all need to rest."

Rhys tore himself away, winced at the pain, clutched at Hugh's hand. "I'm not leaving him!"

"C'mon now," the doctor tried again. "You can't open your stitches again."

Hugh put his hand over Rhys's. "Go on. Go back to sleep."

Rhys slumped onto his knees, but the doctor picked him back up, helping him towards the door, and the fight in Rhys fizzled. He made a halfhearted attempt to stop him, and the doctor paused for a moment, long enough for Rhys and Hugh to meet the other's gaze.

The doctor had to bear most of Rhys's weight as he nearly lost his footing. His face contorting around a sob, Rhys looked at Elena, still standing there in the corner.

"You'll stay with him?"

"She should—" The doctor stopped when Elena's eyes, steely and fierce, flicked to him. The doctor cleared his throat.

She nodded. "Go."

Rhys looked at Hugh one last time, his mouth open to say something but nothing coming out.

Hugh smiled. "I'll see you."

———————

In a harmony that drew tears from Zeneba's eyes, the horns of Karak sung as one, their timbres low, somber, but also hopeful. The smoke of the human fire had been carried away by a strong east wind, and the Red City stood.

When the horns ended their mournful melody,

torches lowered to pyres, set up all around the cliffs. Karak sat in the middle of a circle of burial fire. So many had given their lives.

Zeneba's eyes were transfixed to the west, where her gold and purple standard flapped in a sea breeze. Her hands shook.

Ondra wrapped his around hers and squeezed.

She didn't know if time could heal this wound. The sight of a lifeless Yaro would forever be etched in her memory, but she knew, deep down, that wasn't how she would remember him. No. He had been strong for her, had defended her, her city, her people. That was how she would remember him.

The flames licked up his pyre, small to her eye but she knew it was him. When it was over, when evening lapped onto Karak in lilac waves and all Charneki returned to their halls to look forward to the new dawn, she would take him to the monument, to Zaynab, and lay them together.

For now, though, she told herself to be brave, to stand, unwavering, for him.

Karak herself was battered, her two outer walls almost completely crumbled and many of her facades and halls no more than rubble. But they would rebuild, they would make it better than the ancestors could ever dream. And what was more, they would live.

It had been a momentous effort to organize the city, but she knew it was nothing to its defense and recapture. She couldn't put to words her gratitude to those brave Charneki who had fought to reclaim what was theirs. It gave her a home to come back to. Still, the city had been in near shambles, and before they could think of properly sending all those who had given their lives to the Sunned Ones, she had to see peace and order restored.

There would be much to do after this; the rebuilding project, the human treaty that needed to be negotiated and ratified, and opening talks with the Tikshi would all compete for her attention. But she was determined to see all to fruition. She knew meeting with the Tikshi wouldn't be popular, not after their underhandedness, but she understood that if she wanted lasting peace, it had to be comprehensive. She didn't intend to leave her successor the problems her predecessors had.

"Nahara opens her arms to them," Elder Zhora said softly beside her, his sightless eyes turned towards the Sunned Ones.

"Only she deserves to keep them," Zeneba replied.

As the fires grew large, petals were thrown into the air, strewing the streets in soft blues, pinks, and yellows. Up the great staircase came the two human leaders, the male from the new settlement, and the female from New Haven. Zeneba nodded as they bowed to her, and she was happy to see Cara again.

Cara looked over her shoulder and smiled. From behind her came Rhys, and Zeneba let out a cry of happy surprise. She smiled to see Elena too, who stepped up the stairs and nodded. She took a place next to Ondra and the other Brave Ones.

Rhys took the hand she offered him and came to stand beside her. She had not seen him for some time, having left him behind to recover. Truly she didn't know if he would be able to come today, but she was happy to have him here. It gave her comfort to have him standing with her, and she knew, together, they would meet this new future.

"I am so happy to see you, little one."

"And I you, *mara*."

"You are healing?" she asked.

He smiled, but it didn't reach his eyes. "Yes, *mara*. I am happy to see today."

She clasped his hand tighter. "You are troubled."

His face contorted, holding in tears.

"What is it?"

He shook his head. "Too many died. Many should be here now."

"They did not die in vain." Both she and Rhys looked over at Ondra. He gazed steadily down at Rhys. "Mourn for them, but do not pity them. They gave us this day, and we must honor that."

A ghost passed over Rhys's face.

"We have lost much to this war, you and I," Zeneba told him, drawing his eyes. He nodded. "Two brothers were too steep a price. But I hope now, Rhys, that we might be brother and sister in this new age."

Wiping at his eyes, he nodded. "You would honor me, *mara*."

She smiled down at him. "Then no more tears," she said, though her face was wet with them. "Today is for futures and dawns."

Rhys clutched at her hand, and she returned the squeeze. Slipping her other hand back into Ondra's, Zeneba turned her face into the warm sunlight. Nahara and Undin kissed each of her cheeks. This was their gift to her, this new age. She would make them proud.